AT TAXPAYERS' EXPENSE, six American congressmen pile out of the long, black limo into the classiest whorehouse in Munich. A tall redhead stands in the doorway, flaunting herself in a see-through blouse, moistening her lips with her tongue. Suddenly a shot rings out. Congressman Hurgett falls to the pavement, his head a bloody pulp. A note is found:

"Non, je ne regrette rien."

The following month, Senator Samuels of Michigan dies mysteriously in Italy.
Again a note:

"Non, je ne regrette rien."

BEN SLAYTON: T-MAN has the same reaction as everyone else: "Who is it who has no regrets. What the hell is going on?"

Books by Buck Sanders

BEN SLAYTON: T-MAN #1
A CLEAR AND PRESENT DANGER

BEN SLAYTON: T-MAN #2
STAR OF EGYPT

Published by
WARNER BOOKS

BEN SLAYTON
T-MAN

#1
A Clear and Present Danger

Buck Sanders

WARNER BOOKS

A Warner Communications Company

WARNER BOOKS EDITION

Copyright © 1981 by Warner Books, Inc.
All rights reserved.

Warner Books, Inc., 75 Rockefeller Plaza, New York, N.Y. 10019

 A Warner Communications Company

First Printing: October, 1981

10 9 8 7 6 5 4 3 2 1

BEN SLAYTON
T-MAN

#1
A Clear and
Present Danger

PART ONE

One

He waited, supremely patient, in a tiny, darkened hotel room five stories above the noisy street.

Tonight the drunken fools would come to him unawares. Though the precise hour was irrelevant, the time was indisputably now. The waiting didn't matter. He would be here, they would be down below; and on this night, eventually, history would be made.

He stared at the cobblestone entrance to the square as he smoked. The burning end of a black Tunisian cigarette illuminated his hard-set, determined face. Tonight there was not a trace of fear in those strange, shining eyes, one of which was brown and the other dark green.

Yet once there had been fear in his eyes. Only once, though, a long time ago.

Then, he had been a boy of seven years, which was also the last time he could remember his life being easy. His father had not yet abandoned the family altogether; home was a comfortable flat in a tidy working-class district of Marseilles; and there were frequent holidays in the surrounding mountains and woods of southern France.

On one such occasion, his father had decided to take his son alone, to hunt. He had found himself waiting in a blind then, too.

9

When a huge, heavily antlered buck stepped tentatively into the forest clearing ahead of him, the boy had frozen in some unaccountable terror. He had been unable to pull the trigger.

Behind him, he could feel his father's breath on his neck; he could sense his father's cold anger. The boy had been ashamed, humiliated just as if his father had caught him masturbating.

"Kill him!" his father had hissed.

The buck's nostrils flared and his ears twitched and the animal focused all senses toward the blind, alert to the slightest presence of danger.

"Kill him, you sniveling bastard!" his father hissed again.

The buck's knees bent, positioned for flight. But the animal, too, was frozen with fright. The boy felt a numbness and then a fire in the armpit that held the butt of his rifle stock. His hands felt heavy and icy. There was a thudding sound in his head. Then an explosion.

At first, the boy thought his skull had somehow detonated. Then he saw the thick spray of maroon blood shower the air of the forest clearing beyond the sights of his rifle, the ugly black hole between the buck's fear-crazed eyes; the buck crumpling in sudden death. He had killed with a single, clean shot; his first shot and his first blood.

Something had taken the boy through that momentary stark fear. Now something in him reveled. The boy felt a deep and primal satisfaction move swiftly through his body. His skin glowed, his breath came in rushes, his lips pulled back in a triumphant grin. He felt a tingling in his testicles.

Nothing he had experienced, before or since, was more sublime than that first kill, even though it was only a deer. . . . He tamped out his cigarette and lit another.

How many animals and how many men had he killed since the age of seven? And what was the difference? He grinned.

Returning his eyes to the street leading into the square, now completely clogged with Oktoberfest celebrants, he thought of another moment in the past: sixteen years and eleven months ago, also in a crowded plaza, in the American

10

city of Dallas; another man, much younger than he, waiting in a room with a gun.

He stroked the chill steel of his weapon, a Mannlicher-Carcaño 6.5-millimeter. The same Spanish rifle the man in Dallas had used.

Only this time, he thought, the Mannlicher-Carcaño would not bring about an end. This time, it would bring about a beginning.

He grinned and continued to wait.

"You must point them out to me, Frederick. You all look to me like penguins, black and white and waddling little fellows."

Then she laughed. It was a husky, low laugh, the sort of laugh that came from the lips of a woman who has drunk whisky every night for many years in the course of her professional life.

She was speaking with a man named Heinz, a very short and very sweaty bald-headed functionary of a leading West German trade association. They had known one another for almost a decade on a strictly business basis, which had convinced her that he was a contemporary eunuch, a sexless attendant of other men's women.

Heinz wore a tuxedo, as did all the other men in the ballroom. The other women present were, for the most part, overweight and dour and married to the host Germans, a few hundred of Munich's burghers.

Also in the assembly were a few federal government lights in from Bonn, a half-dozen movie stars from Berlin, as well as a sprinkling of athletes. But virtually no unattached women. Even if there were women available, they could certainly not be attracted to the three men across the room to whom Frederick Heinz was discreetly pointing.

She sighed when she saw them. Typical clientele. Middle-aged to doddering American politicians on a junket. She got them all, sooner or later. Once she had visited Washington and found, to her great surprise, that a good percentage of American politicians were actually handsome men. Why did these men never seem to make their way to her?

11

"I see them," she said to Heinz. "The usual swine."

"Madame Vilbel, you will please mind your tongue! These men are important to us. In America, they occupy great position in—"

"Oh, Frederick, don't be so political," she interrupted. "You're a pimp and nothing more, and I love you just the way you are."

Heinz wiped his brow and the top of his head with a handkerchief. "There is a difference, *leibchen*, between a politician and a pimp?"

She laughed again and kissed his pate.

"You will see to it our visitors are properly entertained," Heinz said. "And you will be remunerated in the customary fashion."

Before she left his side, Madame Vilbel leaned down and pinched Heinz on the left buttock.

On the opposite end of the room, the three Americans talked among themselves. The heftiest of their number spoke:

"You ought to see the way the common folk carry on this time of year in Bavaria. Jesus, it'll run shivers down your goddam spine, I'm telling you. They get into the whole atavistic business of jumping around bonfires in their goddam lederhosen and if some guy in a silly-ass brush of a mustache was to stop by and tell them to kill the first Jew they see around, then goddam but that's what they'd do!"

"So, what's so bad about that?" another of the Congressmen said, doubling over with laughter and causing the same reaction in his colleagues.

"How about another drink?" the third man slurred.

"Heads up, boys," the first man said, the fat one. "I do believe the entertainment committee is upon us, bless her heart."

Madame Vilbel approached, smiled professionally, and took the fat man's extended hand, which he kissed in elaborate continental style. It didn't happen often any more, not after so many years and so many men, but Madame Vilbel felt a quick surge of revulsion. She shook it off.

"You should like to see the city tonight, *ja*?" She looked

each man in his glazed eyes. "Munich is at its best in October, and I am at your service, gentlemen. Shall we continue the evening at my place?"

The three Congressmen agreed. The fat one, who felt compelled to introduce himself—"Barlow Hurgett, ma'am! Representing the noble Ninth District of the great state of South Carolina, the Grand Old Party, and the Moral Majority, yessiree!"—took her by the arm and led the way out of the room and the building.

In the floodlit drive a Mercedes-Benz limousine waited, a chauffeur at the ready. Madame Vilbel nodded to the man behind the wheel. The four piled into the big car, and then without a word of instruction, the chauffeur pulled out into the street and sped down the autobahn toward Schwabing, the city's bohemian quarter.

Schwabing was a district of quaint old public squares, several beer gardens favored a half-century ago by an Austrian émigré born with the name Schickelgrüber, cheap hotels presently favored by transients who put a premium on privacy and a neighborhood tolerance for establishments such as that run by Madame Vilbel.

Off the autobahn and now on the city's surface streets, the going was slow. Throngs of beer-swigging, horn-blowing merrymakers stalled vehicle traffic, sometimes turning entire streets into gigantic open-air parties. The din and the drunkeness would grow louder and wilder before the dawn, which was what the man waiting in the window was counting on.

The Mercedes finally made its way into the square. Its slow pace was followed through the telescopic lens clamped to the end of the Mannlicher-Carcaño's barrel.

The Oktoberfest mob was essentially good-natured, and allowed the limousine to glide through its numbers after a mere twenty minutes of attempting to tip it over.

It stopped at the curb in front of a narrow brownstone. The chauffeur jumped out and opened the rear door. Madame Vilbel emerged first.

The man in the window removed her from his sights,

lowering the rifle a half inch to capture the next exit in telescopic field.

Congressman Barlow Hurgett stepped out and tripped on the curb, landing face down on the sidewalk. Madame Vilbel and the two other Congressmen laughed wildly at the spectacle.

The man in the window drew a bead on the broad, prostrate body. He inched the cross hairs to that exact spot between the clavicles that he knew from long experience was where a bullet would do the most efficient work.

Gently, steadily, he squeezed the trigger. Then even before the bullet slammed into its target, he knew it would be true. He felt the tingling warmth spread through his body, the deep satisfaction of his kill.

And he remembered: Only once had such a mission failed.

In the darkness of the square, in the cacophony of the boozy Oktoberfest night, the crack of a rifle and an American Congressman's instant death would go unnoticed for many crucial minutes. He had no need to hurry.

He watched from the window as Barlow Hurgett's brethren stepped over him, laughing and joking, he supposed, about the ludicrous appearance he made, sprawled as he was in a Munich gutter halfway between a limousine and a whorehouse. And he thought perhaps he could make out madame's throaty laughter.

He grinned. Then he lit a black cigarette and held it in his lips while he used both hands to break down the Mannlicher-Carcaño and pack it away in an unobtrusive case. He did so carefully, almost reverently.

In the dim light of the cigarette, he located the single spent shell. He picked it up off the floor and placed it carefully on the window sill. Then he reached into a shirt pocket and removed a small slip of paper, which he rolled into a cylinder and stuffed inside the conspicuously placed shell.

He left the room then, making his way slowly down the central staircase of the old hotel.

When he reached the street, nothing seemed out of the ordinary, though he knew that soon there would be shrieking and panicked running, and police whistles.

As he left the square, he heard the muffled sounds of a siren in the distance.

Two

Madame Vilbel wept. Her face was a series of hideous black-and-blue lines made by rivers of mascara and eyeliner. The harsh white light of a police torch shone on her, heightening the ghastly appearance.

Barlow Hurgett's two Congressional companions stood bug-eyed and trembling as police went about the customary tasks of preserving a murder scene for forensic examination: chalking the outline of the body, pushing ghoulish onlookers back beyond a barrier of sawbucks, searching windows and rooftops for any unusual activity, taking names, and trying to make sense of initial statements.

The Congressmen were confused further by the fact that everything was playing in German.

One of them said, "We don't say anything until the Embassy sends us lawyers." Hearing this, the other man soiled his trousers.

A police photographer danced around the body, quickly shooting the bloody scene before the medics would drag away his subject. The photographer knew the fat man at his feet was dead, but nevertheless he would have to be quick about his work. Medics threw a fit when he asked for more time for all his shots, even when he was obviously photographing a corpse. As if anything could be done for the corpse!

Another police car arrived, this one unmarked by flashers and sirens. A plainclothesman stepped out the passenger side of th' front seat and made his way through the tight knot of curious locals.

He spoke briefly to the chauffeur of the Mercedes limousine, who demonstrated with gestures how the American had stepped out of the Mercedes and then seemed to trip and fall, face down.

The detective continued listening to the chauffeur while looking toward the upper windows of a hotel across the square from Madame Vilbel's.

Every window was lit, he noticed, except one. The fifth floor. Not only was that particular window dark, he saw, but it was halfway open to the chill night air.

The detective signaled to a pair of uniformed officers, pointed to the window, and said, "We're going up."

An extremely nervous concierge turned over a house passkey to the policemen after telling them, honestly, that he had no clear idea of who held the room on the fifth floor.

"This kind of place," the detective joked with the officers as they scaled the staircase, "employs people who don't notice a thing."

The detective was not surprised to find the room empty. He was, however, surprised to find so conspicuous a piece of evidence as the cartridge shell on the window sill.

Frowning with curiosity, he took a small leather pocketbag from its place on his shoulder, zipped it open, and removed a tweezers and a glassine packet in which to drop this clue. The police laboratory would give it a closer look in the morning.

But then he noticed the paper cylinder inside the shell. He fished it out, gingerly, using the tweezers. He unrolled it and read:

Non, Je Ne Regrette Rien!

The uniformed officers watched as he examined the bit of paper. Then the German detective shrugged, and said to his colleagues, "I don't know what this is, men. I don't happen to read French."

Three

Andreotti DiNicolini told his American visitors that he had something special for them.

He rose from the table and snapped a finger at the ubiquitous steward, who glided over from his station to refill glasses. The steward poured carefully from a linen-wrapped blottle of *Château La Mission Haut Brion,* vintage 1928.

Crossing from one corner of his massive office suite to the other, DiNicolini wondered if his rivals at Renault-Dauphin had served the Americans so sumptuously; he wondered, conversely, if he were treating them too generously at this stage. How does one know, after all, how to properly grease a deal with Americans, the Americans being so righteous about such commonplace European business expenses?

DiNicolini wanted this merger and he would do anything —absolutely anything—to see it through. The wine and these cigars, he thought, as he opened a Moroccan-bound humidor at the edge of his marble desk, were trifles. And so were the women he might be expected to deliver—unless these two wanted men, a situation he had encountered in the course of doing business more than once lately. The real worry would come when the Americans began hinting about off-the-books cash transactions.

But these days, DiNicolini figured, what with the "Abscam" business he'd been reading about in the international press, perhaps he didn't have much to worry about when it came to cash payments. At least, the demands would be somewhat reduced.

Andreotti DiNicolini, the dashing young director of international development for Fiat Motors Italia, Ltd., might soon take his place among the industrial heroes of Western Europe if only he could bring this one off. If only he could duplicate what the French had accomplished last year, a limited partnership with American Motors Corporation. Duplicate, hell! DiNicolini would do considerably better than Renault. He would merge Fiat with one of the American "Big Three" automakers! He, Andreotti DiNicolini, would oversee the merger of Fiat with Chrysler Corporation!

The conditions were exactly right for such a deal. The movie actor the Americans had just elected as their President had given a highly unfavorable response to a reporter's question about continued government loans and loan guarantees for Chrysler; the city of Detroit, Turin's sister "Motown," faced the desperate possibility of thousands more workers out of jobs, a grim prospect for a city in the throes of the highest unemployment rate since the Great Depression of the 1930s.

DiNicolini's task was to convince his two visitors that only in merger could the real competition be effectively challenged—the Japanese competition.

He was confident that he could swing one of the visitors to his way of thinking. That would be Richard Samuels, member of the U.S. Senate and, according to some voices in the American press, the logical Democratic challenger to Ronald Reagan in 1984. And besides, DiNicolini had reason to believe that Samuels had profited personally and rather significantly from the Renault-American Motors deal.

But the other man would be a difficult case, despite (or maybe because of) the fact that he was an Italo-American, Frank Riggio by name. Riggio was chairman of the board of Chrysler, a progressive businessman who was, unfortunately, scrupulously honest. How he had gotten so far was beyond DiNicolini's understanding. How Riggio had gotten so far in the automobile business was beyond anyone's understanding.

The steward stepped out of DiNicolini's path as he returned to the table at which the Americans sat.

"Anything more?" the steward asked.

DiNicolini pointed to his own glass and the steward filled it. Then, when DiNicolini gestured to the ashtrays, which contained the remains of one cigar per man, the steward allowed the slightest trace of a grin to interrupt his poker face.

The steward carefully stacked the ashtrays on his serving tray and stared at them oddly as he backed away from the table. Before disappearing into the pullman kitchen that was part of the office suite, DiNicolini said to him, "Some espresso, Anthony."

DiNicolini looked to the faces of his guests, who agreed that espresso would indeed be the fine finishing touch to the meal they had just completed and the wine they had drunk. He looked again at the steward.

"Right away, please."

Anthony nodded and backed through the kitchen door.

"Now then," DiNicolini said, attending to his guests once more, "here is what I promised."

He extended his hand, which contained a pair of crisply wrapped Individualés, which Senator Samuels correctly gauged at ten dollars a copy. Riggio mumbled an appreciation and struck a match.

"I'll just put this one away for now," Samuels said, tucking the cigar into an interior pocket of his coat. "That is, if you don't mind?"

Riggio and DiNicolini were both already happily puffing away on theirs. Riggio shrugged his shoulders and DiNicolini swept his right hand through the air, dismissing Samuels from any obligation to participate in the smoking ritual.

"Had one already, as you know," Samuels said. DiNicolini detested Samuels' habit of beginning every sentence with a verb.

"Clogs up the heart, absolute murder," Samuels continued, "or so says my doctor. Can't have more than one stogie a day and my ration's up, see. Got to save room for the caffeine."

DiNicolini smiled pleasantly at the Senator as he wondered how much cash it would take to buy him. Whatever, it would be worth the investment. Samuels might very well be President in four years. And why not? The Americans had been proving for years that they were capable of electing absolutely anything to the highest office in the land.

"Coffee, now that's bad, too," Samuels prattled on, "but since I had just one cup of that, and that was way back early in the morning, well, I suppose I can manage that espresso stuff now in the afternoon.

"When in Rome, you know, and all that."

Samuels thought this last remark particularly funny and began snorting and laughing simultaneously.

Riggio shifted uncomfortably in his chair, clearly bored by his fellow American's small chat. If there was business to be done, then by god let's get at it, he thought. He had a fair idea of what DiNicolini would propose, of course, and he knew he had no choice but to consider it. In fact, his only objection at this point of the game was the presence of Samuels, a necessary evil in the age of enabling legislation.

Samuels would be needed to introduce a variety of Congressional bills for whatever business context it would take to salvage the Chrysler Corporation. It would make Samuels a hero in the eyes of the national liberal constituency for bringing about a quasi government-industry partnership, and it would make Samuels a hero in the more immediate constituency of Michigan, where his actions could save thousands of jobs. Also, the deal would fatten Samuels' Swiss accounts. What a racket!

DiNicolini, of course, was thinking the same thing. He said to Samuels, "We shall have the espresso soon, Senator."

Riggio could take it no longer. "How will your government react to what you are about to propose?" he asked, jarring DiNicolini from insignificant concern.

DiNicolini cleared his throat.

"What I am about to propose, Mr. Riggio, is a matter which is easily soluable insofar as it may concern the Italian government, as there is, practically speaking, no such thing as an Italian government," DiNicolini said.

He was pleased to hear Riggio laugh.

"Should we merge our operations," DiNicolini continued,

"or at least a part of them, which, I can clearly tell, is what you have correctly anticipated as my proposal, my government will be only too happy to endorse the enterprise.

"This I can guarantee you, Mr. Riggio. As I said, we have virtually no government. The Queen of England is due here this week, and no one in Rome can think of whom she should see. No one is able to determine who is head of state."

Riggio laughed again.

DiNicolini finished his wine and said, "You may laugh, but this is the truth. In Italy today, someone like your Jimmy Carter would be considered politically charismatic." He looked toward the kitchen door. Where the devil was the steward?

"Don't sweat the Congress," Samuels chimed in, directing his comments to Riggio. "Been over that path before, right?"

A bit of ash fell off Riggio's Individualé. He cupped a hand and caught it. He looked about somewhat helplessly for an ashtray.

"Sorry," DiNicolini said. He rose from the table, now angered by the steward's slowness. "I'll get those ashtrays."

Inside the kitchen, Anthony hurriedly finished what he was doing as he heard DiNicolini's words and his approaching footsteps. Sweat trickled down his back, beneath his starched steward's jacket.

DiNicolini pushed through the door, brusquely, and came face to face with his steward, who held a coffee service in a tray, along with clean ashtrays.

"Sir?" Anthony asked. It appeared to his employer that nothing was amiss.

"Well . . . just carry on."

DiNicolini turned then and reentered the dining area of his suite, briefly embarrassed at having engaged in the triviality of checking Anthony's progress. He was still uneasy with Anthony. The old fellow who had been his steward for so many years had unexpectedly resigned one day a month ago, suggesting that his nephew, Anthony, fill in. He had heard the other day from Anthony that the old fellow had unexpectedly died in his sleep.

DiNicolini resumed his seat at the dining table. Anthony

placed an ashtray near Riggio. He set the other between DiNicolini and the nonsmoking Senator, then circled the table to serve each man a demitasse of espresso.

As Riggio and DiNicolini talked business, and as Samuels mentally calculated his fee for bringing the two industrialists together, the steward quickly returned to the small kitchen.

Once inside, Anthony opened a cupboard and removed a black leather briefcase. From it, he took a suitcoat that matched the dark trousers he was wearing, a pair of brown tortoise-shell glasses, a false mustache, a charcoal gray Borsalino, and a somber four-in-hand.

He removed his steward's jacket and bow tie, placing these items neatly into a drawer where they were customarily stored. Then he patted the mustache into place with a drop of spirit gum. The necktie, suitcoat, and glasses went on next. He now looked every inch the properly uniformed European businessman.

He inspected the kitchen, giving it a final going-over, for he never would return. Everything was in order, everything spotless. He placed the laboratory instruments he had been using into the briefcase and snapped it shut.

The Borsalino in one hand and the briefcase in the other, he left DiNicolini's suite through the kitchen door that connected with a private corridor leading to the main hallway of elevators and offices of lesser men.

At the ground floor, Anthony placed the Borsalino on his head, obscuring his face with the motion as he passed by the checkout guards. They paid little attention to faces, he knew. But like his commander, Anthony was a careful man in such seemingly small matters.

He touched two fingers to his hat brim in salute to the guards at the door, who held open the portals, obliging his perfectly inconspicuous exit from Fiat Motors Italia, Ltd.

He saw her waiting in the first row of the visitors' parking lot, waiting in her dark green Maserati, a shade of emerald that matched her eyes. Sigrid was very tall, very blonde, and extraordinarily beautiful; if only she weren't *his* property, he thought.

She popped open the passenger door and he stepped into

the Maserati, giving her a peck on the cheek as if greeting his wife after a long day's work.

"The telegram?" he asked as he shut the door behind him and she fired the motor.

"I sent it, of course," she said. Her voice carried a light German accent.

She turned the car out of the parking lot.

Richard Samuels wore the look of a man contented by a day full of shrewd business successes. As well he should. The meeting had gone very well with DiNicolini. He knew that Riggio would eventually fall into line on the deal, he had been assured by one of DiNicolini's flunkies that he would be contacted by someone from Fiat before leaving Italy, which Samuels understood to mean payment, and now, en route by the wonderful train Mussolini had built connecting Turin to Rome, he was headed to the warm comforts of the little lady waiting at the hotel. The little lady was not his wife.

A porter knocked on the door of his compartment. Samuels gave him permission to enter.

"Anything I can get you, sir?" the porter asked.

Samuels took his eyes from the window. There was nothing more to be seen now. Darkness had fallen over the landscape.

"A brandy," he told the porter.

Samuels settled back into the banquette and thought about lighting up his cigar when the brandy came. He also thought about money and the day he would become President. Then he felt the stabbing pain in his chest.

It was as if someone were in the train compartment with him, a big knife in hand, the knife jammed into the left side of his chest.

Then he couldn't breathe.

Unable to move his left arm, Samuels grasped at his chest with his right hand as he struggled for air. He fell forward off the banquette. His face hit the floor. Blood trickled out his nostrils. He rolled on the floor, landing finally on his back.

He tried to call out. He could hear his screaming, but he knew no one else could.

His only thought was the length of time it would take for the porter to return.

Sigrid slowed the Maserati to a crawl and joined the long line of automobiles at the border checkpoint. She looked into the rear view mirror, unconsciously checking the suitcase she had packed earlier in the day. It contained weekend clothing and related items for a man and wife off on a brief holiday to Austria. Anthony's briefcase and business suit, as well as the mustache and the glasses and Borsalino, had been disposed of along the highway.

They had no special difficulty getting past the Italian border police.

A clerk in the telegraph office of the Turin train station looked in her international code book and found the number sequence necessary to transmit a message to a place called Chevy Chase, Maryland, United States of America.

She punched up the appropriate computer signals on the transmitter, and when the video screen indicated the channel was open, she studied the slip of paper and carefully tapped out a five-word message.

Four

"Mrs. Richard Samuels?"

The voice on the telephone was foreign and very distant. That did not seem the least bit curious to her. But the fact that it was a man's voice did. Most of the international operators were women.

"This is she."

She next expected to hear her husband's voice.

"We are sorry to disturb you at this hour . . ."

She looked at her wristwatch. It was nearly midnight. She swiftly calculated the time in Italy, a five-hour differential. It was already the next day in Rome.

". . . but this is an emergency," the man said.

"I am afraid, Mrs. Samuels, that we have very sad news for you . . ."

She sat down. She listened only slightly, hearing the man on the other end of the line introduce himself as Inspector Somebody of the so-and-so division of the Roman police. He spoke on as she anticipated everything.

Her eyes were dry and her mind was crystal clear. She had known this moment would come, sooner or later. There were days when she wished the call would come right then and there, so that she could be on with her life. She and her husband had long ago fallen out of love, of course, as per the usual course of marriages in high-level Washington. But she

27

respected him, in spite of his considerable and all-too-human shortcomings. Besides, Richard Samuels had built up quite an impressive insurance portfolio during the last twenty years. That and his Congressional pension, plus widow's benefits . . .

"... and so, you will be receiving official written confirmation within the next few hours, Mrs. Samuels. My personal condolences to you, and may Godspeed."

She managed a thank-you and then made herself a drink, a double bourbon and soda. When she had drunk half of it, she went to the secretary, slid open the center drawer, and reached for the personal telephone directory. It was next to his pistol, a little .22-caliber that had never been fired. She knew she might be finding such curious evidences of his life for the next several months, finding them at unsuspecting moments. A tear came.

She opened the directory to the W's and found the number of her dear old friends, the Winships. Richard and Hamilton had not been friendly for the last several years, though both men were close-mouthed about it to their wives. Each wife, of course, understood the problem. Hamilton Winship hadn't had the time of day for Lyndon Johnson, either, and Richard Samuels had learned all he knew of Washington politics and Washington money from Lyndon. But now all that had died with Richard. She needed to drink tonight with old friends, to drink to Richard's better memory. Edith and Hamilton would come over, even at this hour. They would understand.

Before she could pick up the telephone receiver to make the call, the phone rang. This time it was local.

"Mrs. Richard Samuels?" a man's voice asked.

"Yes."

"Western Union, ma'am. We have a message for you from Turin, Italy."

"Yes."

The man hesitated.

"I read a little French," he said, "but my pronunciation might not be accurate. The message is in French. That's the way we were told to give it."

She didn't know what to think.

"Should I go ahead? Mrs. Samuels?"

28

"Yes," she finally said. "Go ahead with the message." She neither read nor spoke French. What could this be? Now there was no question in her mind but that she must call the Winships. Hamilton especially, since he worked with these mysterious things all the time in his capacity as special deputy secretary of the Treasury Department.

The man from Western Union cleared his throat. Then he said:

"Non, je ne regrette rien."

Five

LONDON, England, 22 January 1981

Ben Slayton sat alone at a table in his favorite saloon, a place called Mother Punch's Ale House. It was situated in the cellar of a squat warehouse in Old Seacoal Lane, just off bustling Fleet Street.

Slayton liked Mother Punch's because it was usually full of talkative journalists, whose company he both enjoyed and found occasionally useful. Besides which, Mother Punch's was a fair distance from the American Embassy, and the only attraction there was shop talk. Slayton had long ago learned that the American Embassy in any country was the worst possible place to learn anything about the host nation. So there was nothing Slayton liked more when assigned abroad than to nip out to some place warm and dark and wet to listen and learn.

Over the past half-dozen years he had been with the U.S. Treasury Department as a troubleshooter agent, Slayton had traveled through dozens of foreign countries; and by his insistent mingling with all classes of people, from the poorest workers and peasants to the bejeweled, he felt he had grown particularly effective in his work.

The fact that he was fluent in French, Spanish, German, and Russian helped his minglings, as did the fact that he was handsome in an average sense, in a pleasant, Middle Western sense, reflecting a secure and rooted upbringing.

31

He was just under six feet in height; a trim but muscular 170 pounds, the build of a light heavyweight boxer; and his dark brown hair, light brown eyes, and narrow facial features told of his German and English ethnic makeup.

He was thirty-five years old, an age when he was beginning to discover how much he didn't know, despite an impressive scholastic background at the University of Michigan and his experience as a much-decorated fighter-bomber in the U.S. Air Force during the Vietnam War, a stock car racer, a collector of vintage automobiles, a collector of contemporary art and literature, a Korean martial arts black belt, and the ability to hold his own at diplomatic dinner parties in Washington. The truth was, he more than held his own. Ben Slayton was always invited, and it was difficult to tell whether the women liked him more than the men, or vice versa.

"So if I'm so damned charming and all," he thought, as he waited for his food and drink, "what am I doing assigned to the Vice Presidential Secret Service detail?"

Slayton had plenty of objections to the bureaucratic pettifoggery of the Treasury Department—and Washington in general—but he always obeyed his superiors, though he would always make his objections well-known following an assignment. It could be worse, he realized. A friend of his had been posted to the Nixon detail. All the poor sap did these days was sit around the former President's fifteenth floor office suite in New York's Federal Plaza and read magazines.

When he originally hired on with the Treasury Department, Slayton was assigned to the Alcohol, Tobacco and Firearms Division—the "action" division, as all T-men called it. His father, a retired police chief in Ann Arbor, Michigan, had wangled the job for him, working through a Congressman pal. Despite the fact that Slayton had come home from the Vietnam War and objected to it vehemently, Slayton was hired. His superiors shifted him all over the Department almost immediately, a rigorous breaking-in period of several years, more rigorous than most T-men receive. Slayton had worked the Customs Bureau, the Internal Revenue Service, and even the Bureau of Foreign

Asset Control, in addition to A.T.F. and the Secret Service, where he was currently assigned.

"Troubleshooter agent," Slayton soon learned, wasn't as impressive as it sounded. He was vaguely worried about his career, worried mostly that he wasn't being noticed as he felt he should.

And though he'd been in a favorite city for only a few days, Slayton would gladly trade London for a long weekend at home, on his beloved farm in Mount Vernon, Virginia, just outside the District of Columbia.

He looked out the window at the fine gray sleet of the London winter day. His reverie was interrupted by the boisterous approach of the publican, his arms laden with plates of hot and cold meats, blood sausages, cheese, and pâté. Slayton shoved the newspapers he had just purchased to a corner of the table to make room for his late-morning repast, which he downed with two pints of Whitbread.

As he ate, he perused the London press, one paper at a time. Rupert Murdoch's *Sun* published the photograph of a particularly bare and buxom "Wakey-Wakey" girl on page three; the *Daily Express* prattled on about Ted and Joan Kennedy's divorce plans; the *Daily Mail* managed to make a hair-raising kidnap yarn over in Dun Laoghaire sound as exciting as a milk carton; and the *Times* was mostly concerned with news of how it would soon fall under the ownership of the very same Murdoch who printed all that trash and flash in the *Sun*. Slayton could almost hear the cursing and shouting that would take place in Mother Punch's a few hours hence when the *Times*men and their compatriots on the city's other legitimate newspapers, the *Observer* and the *Guardian*, began to gather for drinks.

Slayton examined the rest of the *Times*. Page one carried a feature about Ronald Reagan's first two days in the White House and a longish piece about how the American hostages held 444 days in Iran received something less than hospitable treatment. Slayton figured as much. The Moslem yahoos in charge of Teheran these days had only recently begun walking erect. He wondered if there were anything in the way of Iraqi war bonds he might invest in.

But where was the news that was responsible for bringing him here to England?

Slayton riffled through the remaining pages of the slim edition of the *Times*. Then he found it, back by the truss ads:

U.S. VICE PRESIDENT GEORGE BUSH TO VISIT MRS. THATCHER "SOON"

From David Crosley
Washington, Jan 21

President Reagan today told members of the press that his Vice President, Mr. George Bush, would "soon" visit Great Britain for talks with Prime Minister Thatcher.

An aide to the new American President indicated that "soon" would mean "within the next few days." He refused to be more specific, giving rise to some speculations here that American authorities charged with protecting government dignitaries were apprehensive about public announcement of international travel plans.

Within the past few months, two members of the American Congress have died while abroad, one of them having been murdered under mysterious circumstances.

A spokesman for the British Embassy here in Washington, however, said the Americans were planning a reception at their embassy in London on Monday evening, January 25. Presumably, Mr. Bush will arrive in London that day.

Though the inexplicable secrecy surrounding Mr. Bush's travels is something of a minor mystery here, there is no mystery about the new American administration's interest in strengthening ties with Margaret Thatcher's Tory government, whose policies are much admired by the conservative Mr. Reagan. . . .

Slayton stopped reading at this point, uninterested for the moment in the partisan political angle of the story. His concern was with the words "inexplicable secrecy."

He had been told nothing about any extraordinary security measures being taken for the Bush visit. He hadn't expected, of course, that the visit would make news of any import. He figured that Reagan was like any other President in his desire to hustle the Vice President out of town as soon as possible; in fact, Reagan, being as old as he was, would be even more anxious to see little of Vice President Bush, a man whose only function in government was to remind the boss of his mortality.

But Slayton's Secret Service assignment was only temporary, what with the change in administrations and all. Maybe that's why he wasn't filled in.

Something might be in the air about this Bush visit, something more than usual. Slayton was both excited and worried.

LONDON, 8:12 a.m., 25 January 1981

The young man tapped on the bullet-proof glass door, seeking the attention of a guard he could see dozing behind a small desk in the lobby. The guard looked up at the noise, a bit stupidly, and rubbed his eyes.

The guard scowled and checked his wristwatch. Then he rose and walked insolently toward the door. He assessed the young man staring at him from the other side. Dumb punk kid in some kind of trouble far from home, and now he wants us to call his mommy and daddy, the guard decided.

"We open at nine o'clock," the guard shouted from his side.

The young man shook his head. He couldn't hear. The guard shouted again and this time the young man understood the muffled words.

"Please!" the young man cried. And he did cry, too. Big, whelping tears poured from his eyes.

The guard guessed he was twenty-one, maybe twenty-two. He looked like they all do: long dirty hair, skinny as a hose, dressed up in surplus Army fatigues, and running around Europe with nothing that couldn't fit in a rucksack.

Couldn't these damn kids find jobs when they graduated from those fancy schools they all went to, the guard wondered? Why'd they have to go gallivanting around Europe all the time, making life miserable for everyone who worked at embassies? How many punk kids like this had the guard seen turn up on the doorstep? God, he was tired of seeing these young snots with their messes that had to be cleaned up.

Big strapping kid like this, and he's bawling like a puking little kid, the guard thought. He'd seen it lots of times before.

The guard unlatched the heavy door and opened it a crack to hear this one's story.

"Thanks," the young man said quickly. "Thanks a lot. . . ."

Good start, the guard thought. At least he knows how to say thank-you. Most of the young punks only knew how to say "shit" and derivations of "fuck." Those two words seemed to constitute half their vocabulary.

"Listen, man, I had to sleep in the park overnight!" Still crying, the young man pointed to the statue of Franklin D. Roosevelt in the little park opposite the American Embassy in Grosvenor Square.

"I was robbed. I haven't got a cent. And I lost my passport and credit cards. . . ."

The guard snorted and thought to himself: That figures; the punk kid fits himself out like some sort of refugee and he travels with credit cards, yet.

". . . and I don't know anybody here in London to help me. I got to get home, man. . . ."

He started crying again. And he rubbed the back of his head. A trickle of blood appeared on his dirty neck.

"Man, I had to sleep outside! I had to walk here, in the middle of the night, and . . ."

"All right, all right," the guard said. "We'll see to everything. Come on in. I guess it will be all right."

The guard opened the door wider and admitted the young man, whose fingers were now covered with blood from the nasty cut on his head.

"I'll just get you situated with someone," the guard said, "someone who might be in early. But you'll probably have to

36

wait until the big cheeses start coming around. Maybe till 10 o'clock or so."

The young man nodded. "Thanks, man. Really, thanks a lot."

"Yeah, kid. Sure thing."

The young man followed the guard down a long corridor to a carpeted reception area. The massive reception desk was held down by a heavyset woman busy pulverizing a typewriter with her lightning quick, hammerlike fingers. She looked up from her work at the bedraggled young man and the guard at his side.

"What'd you drag in here, huh, Henry?" she said.

"Another Little Boy Blue who's lost his horn is all," the guard answered.

The receptionist nodded. She had heard this story a couple of thousand times since she took the job at the Embassy. And she had taken care of matters in every case. No need to bother the brass.

"Sit down." She waved a fleshy finger toward a government-issue brown imitation leather chair at the side of her desk. Then she removed the paper she had been pounding at in the typewriter and replaced it with a government-issue form.

"Okay," she said. "Name. Home town. Father's name."

"Edward Folger. Yonkers, New York. Thomas Folger."

"Lost your passport, I suppose?"

"Yeah. I mean, yes, ma'am."

She typed these bits of information onto the form.

"Oh boy," she said matter-of-factly. Then she stopped typing and sat back in her chair. "Tell me how it happened, Edward."

"Well, I was walking around the City . . . you know, the East End?"

"I know, dearie. That's where it always happens. Go on."

". . . and anyway, I'm just minding my own business, looking around and all. It's still daylight, and there's lots of people around. Out of the corner of my eye, I see a group of maybe eight or ten little girls. Oh, ten or twelve years old, I guess. They're all freckle-faced and in school uniforms. I didn't pay any attention to them.

"Then right when I'm passing them on the sidewalk, they jump out in front of me. Four or five of them are in front, one or two at a side, and the rest in back of me. They've got me completely surrounded in a tight circle. And they're all mumbling something.

"It's confusing as all hell, you know?"

The receptionist nodded.

"And they're raising their hands at me, but I can't see them because they're covered with sweaters. They're all around me, real close in and mumbling, and I can see those hands moving under the sweaters.

"And then, all of a sudden, just as quick as they mobbed me, they step aside. Then in a flash I realize they must be pickpockets! Damn, I never felt a thing!"

The receptionist said, "They're called 'dippers' here, honey."

The young man rubbed his head and winced. His fingers were now caked with dry blood.

"How'd you get that, Edward?" the secretary asked. She was pointing at his head.

"Well, when I realized they must be—'dippers'—I felt in my pocket, in back, and my billfold was gone. I looked and they were running up a side street and then into an alley."

"And you chased them?"

"Sure. My billfold had everything in it. Cash, passport, American Express . . ."

"Never leave home without it."

"Yeah. Well, so I chased them. I mean, I had to get back my cards and passport anyway, you know?"

"Sure."

"And somewhere in that alley, someone hit me over the head. I never did find the girls, let alone the billfold."

The young man wiped at his mouth.

"You want some coffee, Edward?"

"Oh yeah, thanks so much. I'm dying for coffee."

"Better than dying for something else, right, dearie?"

The young man smiled, which brought out a maternal feeling in the receptionist. She waddled away from her desk to a coffee maker, returning with a cup for her charge.

"Now, I'm going to have to check for passport information, arrange to issue you a temporary document, and then I'm going to have to call your parents and see if they're good for your return ticket home," she explained.

"Oh, thanks a lot," he said, a huge sigh of relief escaping from his dry lips.

Then he asked, "Could I wash my face?"

The receptionist took her place behind her desk. She smiled at him and said, "Yeah, I'd like you to wash your face. You'll look a lot better. Men's room's down that hallway."

Folger followed her finger and disappeared from the reception area, leaving her to her typing and telephoning. He found the door to the men's room, but before entering it, he looked behind him to make sure he was alone in the hallway.

Then he walked past the door to the end of the corridor and a pair of large double doors. He cracked a door open. The ballroom beyond was empty.

Folger stepped inside the ballroom and turned immediately to his right. The heating duct he knew would be about six paces right was where it should be, just above the baseboard and set into the wainscoting. He knelt to his task.

He pulled a screwdriver from his rucksack and removed the metal plating of the heating duct. Then he took a small package from the rucksack, along with a roll of black electrician's tape.

He placed the package inside the duct and secured it with the tape. Then he worked at the package with his fingers, expertly. When he was through, he replaced the metal plating.

Then he left the ballroom, washed up in the men's room, and returned to the reception area.

"Looks like everything checks out, dearie. We'll provide your ticket back home. Your father and mother will be waiting for you at Kennedy. Better luck next time," the receptionist said.

"Thanks a whole lot. Really."

The young man smiled as the receptionist finished her typing.

Air Force II, carrying a napping George Bush, was 104 miles off the western coast of Ireland, en route to London's Heathrow Airport.

Six

Hamilton Winship was a man of habit. If it was forty-five minutes past the noon hour, which it was, then it was time to leave his office in the Treasury Building and take a stroll along the Potomac.

He had begun this habit back in the Ford Administration, as he recalled. That was when Edith had started complaining that he ought to get more exercise, in addition to complaining about the weight he had been gaining as a result of the heavy eating and, for Winship, heavy drinking of late.

Winship had his reasons for those indulgences. They helped dull the anxiety, the malaise he could not shake. It was hardly the usual mid-life crisis. Hamilton Winship was sixty-three years old, and the malaise was still with him.

Ever since the call from Dot Samuels—the hysterical call in the middle of the night—the malaise had grown to an abiding stomach ache. Even if he'd wanted a long lunch at the Sans Souci, it woud have been out of the question. His stomach couldn't take it.

And so he strolled along the Potomac. The day was gray and businesslike. A complete contrast from the bright blue skies of last week, he thought, and the bright hopes attendant to a new Administration. On top of it all, the hostages had finally come home.

But today, on the first day of the first full week of the new order, it was gray and businesslike.

Winship looked up in the air. Somewhere, the new Vice President was on his way to England. "Bush," he spat out. He remembered Bush being the head of the Central Intelligence Agency at the time of the Orlando Lettelier assassination in Washington. Had Bush heeded warnings Winship knew he had received, that murder would not have happened. Had Jimmy Carter heeded warnings, the rabble in Iran wouldn't have been able to hold fifty-two Americans for ransom.

Why did they never listen?

Winship shook his head and breathed in the clean, crisp air. "Don't start it up again, old boy," he said to himself, "or they'll booby-hatch you for sure this time."

Still, he knew he was right. He knew that someone should be reading the warning signs. He thought about Bush en route to England, about the order he had issued against specific announcements regarding his travel schedule. Of course, he noticed how Bush's schedule had been leaked anyway. So much for the authority of a Special Deputy Secretary of the Treasury.

He thought, too, of the senseless assassination of that bourbon-belt Congressman over in Germany. What was his name? Hurgett. Barlow Hurgett. Didn't anyone in the South have any sense when it came to naming their children?

The message left behind in the Hurgett murder had been classified, of course. Which meant that another warning would go unheeded, would be stashed away on some shelf somewhere.

And the same message in the death of Senator Richard Samuels, only telegraphed. Winship had taken it from Samuels' widow, Dorothy, and kept it in his own private files.

What would he do with his files? His suspicions?

He thought back to the days of his prime as a T-man, back to the specific day which had begun Winship's long nightmare. . . .

It was the twenty-second of November, 1963. Hamilton

42

Winship, a high-level operative in the intelligence unit of the Secret Service, was at work in his Treasury Building office. His friend, the young President John F. Kennedy, was flying today to Dallas, Texas, along with Vice President Johnson.

Winship had been meeting frequently with Kennedy over the past week. The President had confided to Winship and certain others in the intelligence community that he was dissatisfied with John McCone, his head of C.I.A., and with the C.I.A. itself. Both McCone and the agency were "insubordinate bordering on treasonous," the young President said, though in a different way. McCone was simply unable to bring into line the C.I.A., the "Company," as it was called in Washington officialdom.

The old-guard covert operatives, the men who worked with Meyer Lansky and Lucky Luciano and various other hoodlums and *mafiosi* during World War II, especially during the Allied invasion of Sicily, had managed to see their Office of Strategic Services become the C.I.A. The independence enjoyed by the Company was insufferable to men like Winship, whose own Treasury Department had long been in the intelligence business, long before either the C.I.A. or the F.B.I. To President Kennedy, the C.I.A. was more than insufferable. It was a menace.

That day in his office, as the President was flying to the southwest, Winship was working up the report he would have to give to Kennedy upon his return from Texas. The President had asked him to offer suggestions for a major housecleaning in the C.I.A. His exact words had been, "The Company has to be dealt with."

Yet today, as he worked on his report, Winship discovered that in defiance of direct Presidential orders, the C.I.A. had placed operatives in Havana, Cuba, for the purpose of assassinating Fidel Castro. It was a second assassination plot, actually, the first one having failed and resulting in President Kennedy's very specific orders to leave Cuba alone, to leave Castro alone.

The C.I.A.'s defiance was particularly irksome in view of the fact that President Kennedy's emissaries to the Castro government had this very day met with Havana's representatives to open talks toward normalization of diplomatic relations between the United States and Cuba. Winship was on the telephone shouting to his counterpart at the Company when an aide burst into his office, red-faced, his arms waving, his face a study in fright.

Winship thought the C.I.A. goons had carried it off this time, that Castro had just gotten it. But he was wrong.

John F. Kennedy had been shot down in Dallas.

By some perverse instinct, Hamilton Winship decided at that moment to conduct his own investigation, to keep his own counsel. He cleared his desk of the report he was putting together for President Kennedy. Would he ever file it with President Johnson? He couldn't know, at that moment. It was more important to follow the events immediately following the assassination.

As the world mourned, as the world reeled in the shock of the Kennedy assassination, Hamilton Winship used his access to classified documents and his matchless abilities as an investigator to assemble a disturbing set of facts surrounding the case.

Winship found, for instance, that Lee Harvey Oswald, the man arrested for Kennedy's assassination and in a matter of days gunned down by Jack Ruby, a low-level member of a Chicago crime syndicate, had in the late 1950s been given a top security clearance by the U.S. Marine Corps to work at a C.I.A.-sponsored U-2 air base in Japan.

Shortly after winning his top security status, Winship discovered, Oswald defected to the Soviet Union, somehow paying a $1,500 travel fare when his personal bank account held only $203.

In Moscow, Oswald claimed to be a Marxist and said publicly that he intended to give the Kremlin all the military secrets to which he was privy.

However, the Kremlin was convinced that Oswald was a double agent for the C.I.A. Winship learned this from a friend of his who had defected to the United States as a K.G.B. agent.

And so, two years later, in 1962, Oswald returned to the United States a humbled man. Despite his prior admissions of treason, Lee Harvey Oswald was routinely handed back his American citizenship papers.

Furthermore, Winship found that the pro-Castro leaflets which Oswald had been distributing in New Orleans in September of 1963 were stamped with the address of a building used by a C.I.A. front group called the "Cuban Revolutionary Council," an *anti*-Castro organization established during the Bay of Pigs invasion by E. Howard Hunt.

Several cartons full of Oswald's leaflets were discovered in Washington, in the home of Robert Maheu, a former F.B.I. agent who had opened a private detective agency in Washington with the C.I.A. as his principal client. Other of Maheu's clientele included Carlos Marcello, the *capo de tutti capo* of New Orleans' Mafia; and the ubiquitous E. Howard Hunt.

Winship could come to no other conclusion but that Lee Oswald was a C.I.A. operative, probably low-level, who had acted in conspiracy with many others—namely, certain renegade C.I.A. agents and *mafiosi* in New Orleans, Havana and Chicago—to assassinate President Kennedy.

But his conclusions only raised far more pervasive and cancerous questions. How, for instance, had such an outlaw element been allowed to grow in the American intelligence community? Exactly why was Kennedy murdered? Because of his repeated threats to the dangerous insubordination of the C.I.A. and certain high-level F.B.I. officials? Because of his brother Bobby's, the Attorney General's, aggressive prosecution of *mafiosi* in big business and big labor?

Winship requested and received private audience with the new President, Lyndon Johnson. He laid out his horrible preliminary findings and urged Johnson to arrange with Senate leaders to use committee subpoena powers to probe the American intelligence network and its cooperative ties with overseas terrorists—namely, in Havana—and with organized crime.

Johnson heard him out, congratulated him for his diligent patriotism, professed shock and outrage, privately, and never again spoke to Winship.

When the President appointed a blue-ribbon investigatory commission to report on the Kennedy assassination, Winship requested, and received, private audience with its chairman, then Chief Justice of the Supreme Court, Earl Warren.

Warren expressed more private shock and outrage, and then his commission declared that Lee Harvey Oswald was the lone and deranged assassin of John F. Kennedy. The national press gleefully cooperated in this fiction by portraying anyone who thought differently—most especially anyone who suggested conspiracy—as members of the Flat Earth Society.

But Winship continued his agitations, discreetly, well within the Washington confidence circles he had so carefully cultivated all his life. For his efforts, he ceased to be a full member of those circles, and his power and authority dwindled, gradually at first, then mightily toward the end of the first Nixon administration.

Though Watergate was merely a gleam in the strange eyes of G. Gordon Liddy et al, Winship was already on to numerous "black bag" jobs of a highly suspicious political nature being carried out by former or present C.I.A. operatives, including, incredibly, E. Howard Hunt. With little to lose, Winship reported his concerns about the renewed illegal conduct of intelligence agents, and the roof fell in, as it were.

One afternoon, a delegation of top-level C.I.A. officials met with Winship in his office at Treasury. They urged him to keep his "undue fears" to himself. Or else. National security and all that, they explained. Understand?

The threat was accompanied by the next day's promotion to oblivion. Winship's new title was to be "Special Deputy Secretary of the Treasury" with responsibility for recruitment needs. He told Edith that it meant he was head janitor. She cried, then composed herself, and told him, "Hamilton, you have two choices: you can either resign and try to get your story before the public, or you can stick with it, on the inside, and wait for the right combination of circumstances for the truth to triumph."

Good old girl. She was absolutely correct. In fact, Winship had decided on the latter course just before his wife verbalized it.

And he kept dutifully quiet, through it all. A member of the Warren Commission named Gerald R. Ford became President and a two-time assassination target, and Winship kept quiet. In 1979, during the Carter administration, a Con-

46

gressional committee found that a conspiracy "appeared" to have been involved in the Kennedy assassination; Winship kept quiet, knowing that despite this extraordinary acknowledgement by the government, nothing would be done to bring any of the co-conspirators to justice. He was right.

As a result of his good grace and quietude, Winship was readmitted to his circles, though not to any position of power. He could hear all of the confidential business of the nation once more, but he would forever be barred from doing anything about it.

It wasn't entirely difficult for Hamilton Winship to keep himself discreet, for he himself began to wonder, about once a month, whether he was a full-blown paranoid, when all about him his friends and colleagues and countrymen remained underwhelmed by the treachery of so much that he saw in government. Could all those people be wrong? Could he alone be right? Winship developed ulcers. And he waited.

While he waited—for what?—he enjoyed the comforts of socializing with those who controlled Washington and the federal establishment, including the C.I.A., year in and year out, as Presidents came and went. Those were the people just like himself. Eastern-educated and/or bred, discreet, well-married, old boy and old girl.

Winship was a Yale man through and through, born and raised in Westchester County as the scion of an old planter family whose money had long ago been wisely set to work in Wall Street. Edith was his perfect accompaniment—Bucks County, Lord & Taylor, and Wellesley. The two of them were soft-spoken, elegantly witty, cultured, and Georgetown fixtures. Their sedate appearance masked the fact that the two of them held an abiding and passionate affection for one another that had intensified every year of their thirty-five years together. They had always wished for children, even now, in their sixties; their inability to produce children was the tenderest of their sorrows.

In physical appearance, Winship resembled a plump British peer, with a bulky chest and belly requiring a waistcoat at all times, a ruddy tone of skin that proved an enormous fondness for vintage wines, a shock of silver hair brushed straight back from his forehead, and a mustache to match, kept in immaculate trim. In outlook, too, he was pure peerage, someone whose *noblesse oblige* lay in overseeing the government bureaucracy. Someone, after all, had to be born to manage the civil servants.

He liked himself, and he liked the people like him. And yet it pained Hamilton Winship to know, as he had but no choice knowing, that it was *his* sort who benignly neglected the conspiracy to assassinate Kennedy, *his* sort of people who were ultimately responsible for the excesses of the F.B.I. and the C.I.A.

His sort of people were men like George Bush.

Again he thought of Bush en route to England, as he strolled the Potomac walkway.

And this prompted him to think of Hurgett and Samuels, the messages left at their deaths. . . .

Winship stopped dead in his tracks. His face paled. He whirled around, searching out a telephone booth. Then he clutched the collar of his topcoat around his throat to keep out the wind from the river, and ran at top speed.

He nearly stumbled when his foot hit an ice-covered pothole. He paid no heed to his water-covered pantleg and shoe. Winship kept running.

He finally reached the booth and tried to get his breathing under control while he fished through his pockets for coins. He would need all the authority in his voice that he could muster.

And then maybe that wouldn't be enough.

Seven

LONDON, 7:16 p.m., 25 January 1981

A soft mist swirled through amber washes of light from the street lamps. People moved briskly through the dusk, with Burberry coats drawn tight and black umbrellas unfurled. The echo of the last peel from Big Ben, announcing one-quarter past the hour, was a wet muffled sound. London was one of those few cities, along with San Francisco, Brussels, and Paris, made all the more picturesque by gentle rain. All the more mysterious as well.

Ben Slayton picked his way through Dover Street, careful to step around the puddles that had quickly formed on the fashionable but badly chipped and rutted walkway. He didn't wish to spot his formal shoes. He held a newspaper over his head to keep dry. He was on his way to the Embassy at Grosvenor Square, a ten-minute walk from Brown's, the hotel used by Secret Service agents assigned to advance work.

When he reached the Embassy and walked inside, he shook himself, almost as a dog would after a swim in a river. He hung his overcoat in the nearest closet and disposed of the sodden newspaper that had kept his head dry. He checked the Baume & Mercier watch on his left wrist. Plenty of time before the guests would begin arriving.

Slayton nodded greetings to his fellow agents, slouched

against the walls, waiting for the place to fill up with notables and the time they would have to snap to.

"The Veep in yet?" Slayton asked one of them.

"Naw, Sir Prep's plane hasn't even landed."

Slayton laughed quietly. It was the first time he'd heard the appellation "Sir Prep." Of course, every President and Vice President was nicknamed by Secret Service agents. Jimmy Carter was "Mr. Peanut," naturally; Walter Mondale was known as "Fritzy"; Gerald Ford had been "Bozo"; and Nixon was "Tricky" up until the time he left the White House, was pardoned of Watergate crimes, and became "Sir Richard of San Clemency."

Slayton repaired to the men's room on the main floor to check his appearance.

Appearance was important to Slayton. Vital, in many cases, especially when he was assigned to the A.T.F. A man's dress and carriage, he knew, could signal all manner of impressions. It was helpful to control those impressions.

Tonight he was in black tie for the state affair. He examined himself in a mirror. He looked every bit the up-and-coming young diplomat, every bit a man of the world involved in far more intrigue than he would or could let on. Women loved it. Only the tiny earphone and the bright green metallic lapel button betrayed him as a Secret Service agent. Women loved that, too, as he had discovered on more than one occasion.

The point was, he looked as if he belonged. Ben Slayton could just as easily blend in with a gang of Puerto Ricans shooting craps in the South Bronx.

"Is anybody in this outfit besides me ever going to see how fucking good I am at 'my job?" he thought to himself.

Slayton left the men's room, satisfied finally that his dark red tuft of handkerchief in his breast coat pocket and the pearl studs of his snowy shirt were properly aligned. He wondered if he would have to sleep alone tonight.

To his right, down the corridor, was the entrance to the ballroom, where the reception would take place in an hour or so.

"Through with the check list?" Slayton asked of a Secret

Service agent named Nelson who stood by the door filing his nails.

"Yeah," Nelson said, not looking up. "You want to go over it yourself? Help yourself."

Slayton picked up the day's duty sheet from a table. On it were the various Secret Service functions prescribed for that period beginning at 0:00 hours and ending at 24:5999 hours. Each segment of time had to be accounted for, signed and countersigned. Radar sweeps, food inspections, kitchen searches, outside personnel checks, press affiliation verifications, identification tag distribution, and detailed furnishings examination.

All seemed to be in order.

Slayton next perused the check-list column marked "guard watch." He didn't see the customary signatures attesting for a proper guard at the reception room door from 7:30 to 8:30 that morning.

"Look at this, Nelson."

Slayton roused Nelson's attention by shoving the duty sheet below his nose.

"Where's the signatures here?" Slayton was pointing to the sixty-minute morning period.

"Beats me," Nelson said. "We'd better check with Artie."

"Wait here," Slayton said when Nelson started to join him in leaving the reception room doorway to find Arthur Posten, the Secret Service supervising agent. "If there really has been an interruption in guard detail, we don't want to be responsible for another one."

"Yeah," Nelson said. A scribble of worry played across his face.

"It's probably nothing," Slayton said. "But let's play by the book."

"Yeah."

Slayton walked briskly down the corridor to the main lobby of the Embassy building, where he knew he would find Posten. He presented the check list, pointing to the one-hour gap.

"Could this be a mistake, or was the reception room door actually unguarded this morning?" Slayton asked.

Agent Posten studied the paper, made a telephone call to

a subordinate, and slammed down the receiver angrily. His face went red.

"Crocker, my counterpart on the morning watch!" he spat. "Know him?"

Slayton shook his head no.

"Should have retired that old man long ago. Seems he excused one of the agents who called in complaining of the runs, and he forgot to replace him at the post in question. Crocker forgot! Can you believe it? He ought to have his armpits set on fire."

"Where's the visitors list for today?" Slayton asked, ignoring Posten's laughing at his own joke.

"I don't know," Posten finally said, drying his eyes.

"Find it." Slayton's tone was firm, even commanding.

"Just a minute—"

"Find it," Slayton repeated.

Posten was about to draw himself up to full height, which was some three inches more than Slayton, but knew it was a ridiculous gesture. Clearly, Slayton was correct to express concern. This was no time for pulling rank, no time for taking umbrage at the sound of a man's voice.

"Come on," Posten said. Slayton followed the supervising agent to the main reception desk of the Embassy.

"Keys to the desk," Posten told a Secret Service agent stationed near the desk. The agent produced a ring of keys.

From the center drawer, Posten produced a log book. He thumbed open the list of entries for January 25. Slayton checked his wristwatch. He calculated he had fifteen minutes before guests would begin milling about.

Slayton's finger ran down the day's entries. He recognized several of the names. His eye returned to the first name, at the top of the list: Edward Folger.

"This was before opening hours," Slayton said, noting the 8:15 a.m. time of arrival at the desk. "Why?"

Posten took a look.

"Robbery victim," Posten said. "See?" He pointed to the secretary's cramped handwriting.

"Probably slept outside overnight," Posten explained. "It happens all the time. Kids get in trouble and head here when hey haven't got any cash. We get them back home and collect from their parents."

Slayton felt a little sick to his stomach. It passed. He had no time to be less than his most efficient.

"We've got to check this one out, sir," Slayton said.

"I know," Posten said.

Slayton sat down at the receptionist's desk and picked up the telephone. He dialed the Embassy switchboard.

"Get me the home telephone of whoever worked at the main receptionist's desk this morning," he said to the operator. "And put a wiggle on it. This is an emergency."

He replaced the telephone and looked up at Posten.

"Organize a very discreet search," he said.

Posten was about to say something like, "Who's in charge here, anyway?" but thought better of it. Instead, he said, "I'm going to make a very quiet search throughout the building. I want you to let me know what you find out from the receptionist."

"Right, skipper."

The telephone rang. Posten scurried off to attend to his search as Slayton answered.

"Yes?" A woman's voice.

"This is Agent Ben Slayton, Secret Service," he said. "Your name, please?"

"Naomi. Naomi Wyatt . . . why?"

"You were working at the main receptionist desk in the embassy this morning at about eight o'clock?"

"Yes."

"And you attended to someone named Edward Folger?"

"Yes. What is it?"

"Tell me about him."

She did as she was told, relating how the young man had been the victim of pickpockets, how he had shown up at the Embassy penniless and frightened.

"How did you handle the problem?" Slayton asked.

"In the usual way. I telephoned his parents, back in the States, and had them arrange to meet him at an airport near the place of residence, which in this case was, as I recall, Kennedy, in New York. Then I—"

"Is there a record of all this?"

"In the upper left-hand drawer. It's a typed form, about eight-by-ten."

Slayton tested the keys in the lock of the upper left drawer until he found the proper one and opened it.

"Okay, Naomi, I've found it," he said. "Right on top."

"I told you," she said testily.

Slayton ignored the remark. He didn't care about diplomacy.

"Thomas Folger of Yonkers, New York. That's the father's name?"

"Right. I remember it now. The telephone number in the States should be right there on the form."

Indeed it was.

"Tell me, Naomi, what happened when you telephoned Yonkers?"

"Well, it was the middle of the night to them, of course. I woke them up. I explained that their son was stranded in London, and then I asked if they would guarantee repayment if we booked him on the next flight home, and they agreed, and that was that."

Slayton thought for a moment, and then said, "And how long did this Edward Folger stay here in the embassy building?"

"Oh, not long, Mr. Slayton. I was able to get him on a 10 o'clock T.W.A. flight to Kennedy from Heathrow, so he only had time to clean up a bit in the men's room here before leaving for—"

"He used the men's room? Which one?"

"The one down around the corner from my desk."

"There is a men's room near the doorway leading into the ballroom on the main floor of the Embassy. Would that be the one?"

"Yes, that's it."

"Good-bye, Miss Wyatt."

Slayton clicked off. He took a deep breath to calm himself. Then he dialed the Stateside number of Thomas Folger, Yonkers, New York.

There was a scratching at the other end of the line, then some clicking noises and finally a recorded voice:

"We're sorry we are unable to complete your call at this

time. The number you have dialed has been disconnected. There is no new number. . . ."

More scratchings, then the recorded voice repeated the message.

Slayton checked his watch. No time to lose.

He dashed from the receptionist's desk to the corridor, but slowed to a purposeful walk when he encountered the first streams of British dignitaries sweeping into the Embassy, on their way to the ballroom and an evening with the new American Vice President, "Sir Prep."

The ballroom had begun to fill as he entered. Glasses full of champagne began tinkling. Cigarette smoke and small talk filled the air. A pianist was playing something from Gershwin, softly, with just enough volume to start people speaking to one another slightly louder than usual. The Embassy social staff knew all the tricks of the trade.

Slayton masked his frantic feelings. He had to assume the worst, that Edward Folger, whoever he was, was a saboteur. He had left the premises. That much Slayton knew. But had he left a little surprise behind? That was what he feared.

Across the ballroom, Slayton could see Posten. It looked as though the supervising agent was sweating. Posten spotted him and crossed the room.

"What have you got?" Posten asked.

Slayton told him what he had learned from Naomi Wyatt, the receptionist.

"Possible saboteur," Posten said.

"You're telling me."

Both men swept the room with their eyes.

"I imagine you're going to have to evacuate," Slayton said. "Have you contacted Heathrow yet? You can't let Sir Prep in."

Posten slapped his forehead.

"Oh my god," he said. He walked briskly from the room, leaving Slayton to wonder if he had signed on with the Keystone Kops or with the U.S. Secret Service.

Again, Slayton scanned the room. All his training taught him to seek out the most obvious. Better than ninety percent of the time, he had learned from his own investigative experience, criminals would take the easy route.

His gaze fixed on a heating duct built into the wainscoting of the wall. Each wall was so equipped, he further noticed. They would all have to be searched. Slayton walked to the one nearest the entrance doorway.

He knelt down on the floor and peered into the grating of the duct. He could see nothing. He drew a match from his pocket and lit it. He could see only dark shapes inside. Nothing unusual. He pressed an ear to the grating. For a moment, he couldn't tell if he actually heard ticking or imagined he heard it.

Then, with a dull horror and a quickened beat of his own pulse, Slayton realized he had found a bomb.

He looked up. Incredibly, no one in the ballroom paid any heed to his kneeling before the heat duct, his ear to the wall.

Slayton reached into his pocket and removed a pen knife. He opened it and began working at the screws holding the grating into place. The screws came off easily, a further indication that something was amiss. Someone had taken off the grating this day.

A line of perspiration broke across his forehead and upper lip.

Finally, he removed the grating.

There it was, neatly taped into place, softly ticking.

Slayton carefully cut the heavy tape with his knife blade and pulled the square bomb package from the wall. He stood up slowly and covered the bomb with an edge of his coat. Then he began walking out of the ballroom.

A heavy-bosomed society matron watched him as he made his way through the corridor to a service hall leading out through the kitchen to the rear alley.

"I say, young man," she said imperiously, blocking his path. "What have you? What seems to be going on?"

Slayton grinned, just a bit wanly, and sidestepped her.

"The latest in remote control gate-crashing," he told her over his shoulder.

Outside, finally, in the damp chill London air, Slayton set down the bomb. He delicately pulled the bits of brown cloth and paper that covered the package.

Inside, he found precisely what he expected. Dynamite

cylinders connected by fuse to a blasting cap and timing device.

Slayton squeezed the positive terminus of the double fuse, holding it taut between the fingers of his left hand. His pen knife still open, he moved the blade to the fuse and closed his eyes. Gently, he made a slicing motion against the edge of the fuse with his knife.

He felt the fuse sever, and he breathed a deep sigh of relief, knowing that the bomb was now useless.

But blasting caps were not to be trifled with. Slayton's work was not yet finished.

He clipped away all ends of the double fuse, freeing the blasting cap itself from the dynamite. He sank the cap into a three-inch deep puddle of rain water.

Slayton then made his way to the service door.

When he reached the kitchen, he sat down before he fell down. His legs were shaking. His breathing was rapid and irregular.

One of the cooks on duty, noticing how peculiar he looked, approached him.

"Sick?" the cook asked.

Slayton couldn't say anything until he had caught his breath. Then, "Get word to Posten. Arthur Posten, supervising Secret Service agent. Tell him to get his fanny in here to see me."

The cook wasted no time.

In five minutes, Slayton, considerably calmer now, his mind racing with questions about Edward Folger and Thomas Folger and Yonkers, New York, was greeted by an ebullient Arthur Posten.

"Our worries are over," Posten said.

Slayton looked at him incredulously.

Posten continued, "The Vice President has been delayed, by word higher up. His landing was scrubbed. Right now, Sir Prep and Air Force II are sitting quietly at Shannon Airport in Ireland."

"What?"

"I say, the Vice President—"

"Who ordered it scrubbed?" Slayton asked.

"Honcho back in Washington. Hamilton Winship."

Eight

Hamilton Winship sat in his mahogany-paneled office in the Treasury Building, poring over the confidential memo sent to him by a young agent named Benjamin Justin Slayton. Underneath the memo was a manila folder containing a dossier on the memo writer, which Winship intended to read next.

Halfway through the memo, Winship shoved his chair back from his desk and sighed. He took off his glasses, rose from his chair, and paced the floor in his vest and shirtsleeves.

Photographs of Washington and of world notables, all of them shaking hands with Winship, covered those sections of the walls not filled by bookshelves or paintings. He paused as he passed by each of the Presidents he had known in his time—Roosevelt, Truman, Eisenhower, Kennedy, Johnson, Nixon, Ford, Carter, and now Reagan. He had met Reagan for the first time back in 1968, the first time Reagan had been a Presidential candidate, the time when two men armed with Molotov cocktails were arrested by alert California state troopers outside the then-Governor's Sacramento residence.

All of the Presidents had been the target of assassins, Winship mused. The public had known about most of the attempts, though the Secret Service had managed to keep

59

out of the press those attempts against Eisenhower, Johnson, and Carter.

Now this attempt on Bush.

Winship muttered. Bush would keep quiet, he figured. He was an ex-C.I.A. man, so he would keep his mouth shut about this. Thankfully, no press had been on hand when it happened. And the press was still being so polite with the new Reagan-Bush administration that no one thought to ask why Air Force II was mysteriously called down to Dublin, why the Vice President's appearance in London had an unannounced twenty-four-hour delay.

He wanted a drink very badly. Winship felt the old paranoia, which he knew deep down to be a perfectly proper reaction to many of the events he watched from his office, and the simultaneous outrage. Other Americans must feel the same way at times, he thought. One of these days, someone like Lyndon LaRouche was going to be taken seriously. His paranoid constituency would eventually be able to show that someone, somewhere is after us all.

Winship took some small comfort in knowing that men like himself, who ran the intelligence divisions of the Treasury Department, had always worked against the frustrations of an official Washington which refused to be vigilant.

The first refusal to recognize the special vulnerability of Presidents and Vice Presidents came on the tenth of January, 1835. Winship reflected on the history of that day:

President Andrew Jackson was attending the funeral of a South Carolina Congressman in the Capitol Rotunda. One of the mourners was a fellow named Richard Lawrence, who worked his way through the crowd, confronted the President, flung open his coat, and brandished two pistols.

The first pistol failed to fire. Jackson was enraged, and rushed his assailant with the intention of delivering a sound thrashing with his own hands. But Lawrence managed to wriggle out of Jackson's grasp.

Lawrence stepped back and squeezed the trigger of the second pistol. Miraculously, that, too, failed to fire. Andrew Jackson lived.

At his trial a few months later, Richard Lawrence was

adjudged not guilty by virtue of "having been under the influence of insanity at the time he committed the act."

No special action was taken by Congress—or even the Department of the Treasury—to establish a formal bodyguard service for the President.

Then came Lincoln.

In 1861, an operative of the Baltimore private detective agency headed by Allan Pinkerton got wind of a conspiracy involving a group of Southern extremists bent on assassinating the Yankee President as he traveled through Baltimore en route to Washington. The Pinkertons—with absolutely no help from the government—arranged a series of disguises for the President, and managed to switch railway cars, thereby successfully foiling the death plot. That time.

There would be, of course, a bullet for Lincoln. It would come four years later at the Ford's Theatre in Washington, on the evening of April 14, 1865. In that tensest time of the nation's history, a time when assassination plots and assorted other treacherous conspiracies filled Washington's air following cessation of the Civil War, the President was guarded by a single police officer employed by the City of Washington.

That police officer became bored with his duty that fateful night and left the theatre for a nearby saloon. Enter John Wilkes Booth, a man who for months previous to April 14 had told anyone who cared to listen that he was bound and determined to murder Abraham Lincoln.

During the afternoon prior to the evening murder, John Wilkes Booth actually prepared the stage, as it were, for homicide, going about his deadly business with complete freedom from interference by any police agency or police officer. He bored a peephole in the door to the private box reserved by the theatre for President and Mrs. Lincoln; he made certain that the door could not be latched in the normal way from the inside; and he even constructed a device with which he could bolt the door himself after he had gained entry for his murderous deed.

After killing Lincoln with a single shot, Booth injured himself in flight, actually breaking a leg. Even so, the President's security was so lax that a man with a broken limb managed to flee the city in the dark of the night.

But even the assassination of Abraham Lincoln failed to bring about proper and permanent Presidential protection.

Sixteen years later, President James A. Garfield was gunned down in a Washington railway depot some four months after being sworn into office. Like John Wilkes Booth, Garfield's assassin—one Charles J. Guiteau—was a man whose repeated public utterances about assassinating the President should have guaranteed him a prominent place in even the crudest file of individuals to be kept under surveillance and away from the vicinity of the President.

And even this Presidential assassination would not be a catalyst to Congressional action. William McKinley would have to fall.

It was on September 6, 1901, while President McKinley was attending the Pan-American Exposition at Buffalo, New York, that a young anarchist named Leon F. Czolgosz slowly moved through a throng around the President and his party, quietly removed a .32 caliber Iver-Johnson revolver from his belt, and jammed it up against the President's breast bone, firing twice before being beaten senseless by a swarm of local police and a handful of soldiers accompanying the President.

On that occasion, the President's guard had seemed adequate, in terms of the sheer number of men around him, and in terms of accurate intelligence. Twice the schedule for McKinley to receive the public was postponed when his guards heard of anarchist plots to kill him. But McKinley himself refused to cancel his appearance altogether, telling his aides, "Why, no one would want to hurt me!"

Theodore Roosevelt became President upon McKinley's death. He managed to convince the public and the Congress that the Presidency offered the surest route to the grave since Russian roulette, and saw to it that the Treasury Department's Secret Service unit, busied heretofore with the formidable battle against rampant counterfeiting, was assigned the additional task of protecting the President and the Vice President. It became the single most difficult job to be laid before the doorstep of a law enforcement agency anywhere in the world.

Teddy Roosevelt himself would be the victim of an assassin's attempt eleven years after assigning the Secret Service its sobering responsibility. He was saved from death by gunfire when the would-be assassin's bullet was slowed on its path to Roosevelt's heart by a thick manuscript of the speech he carried in his inside breast coat pocket.

In the next few decades, President Franklin D. Roosevelt would nearly be killed by Giuseppe Zangara, whose five shots squeezed off at Roosevelt in a Chicago appearance between F.D.R.'s election and 1933 inauguration managed instead to kill Mayor Anthony Cermak. Zangara, it was learned, had originally intended to kill lame-duck President Herbert Hoover, but decided at the last minute on Roosevelt, as the newcomer would be a handier target.

Following F.D.R., President Harry S Truman would be the target of a pair of Puerto Rican nationalists bent on gaining world attention through assassinating the President. Then Gerald Ford, in the mid 1970s, would twice be the target of assassins, one of whom, "Squeaky" Fromme, had been a member of the Charles Manson murder cult. Richard Nixon would be stalked by one Arthur Bremer, who, like Zangora before him, switched his sights and gunned down Presidential candidate George C. Wallace instead, crippling the former Governor of Alabama for life.

That was the stuff of public consumption. Along with a few other high-level intelligence men in Washington, Winship knew of other attempts not detected by the media.

In June of 1957, for instance, a lunatic inspired by billboards calling for the impeachment of Earl Warren and political tracts which accused President Eisenhower of actively assisting the "international Communist conspiracy," was nabbed on the fourteenth hole at Burning Tree Country Club when Secret Service agents accompanying the President noticed something amiss about the golf bag of an odd-looking man who spent a lot of time in the rough searching for errant balls. Agents discovered a shotgun where a seven-iron should have reposed.

A few months after Lyndon Johnson left office to retire at the Pedernales ranch he had acquired while a high-rolling Senator from Texas, he was fired on from a helicopter as he

63

rode the range of his spread in an open-top Lincoln Continental. The murderous pilot was shot down out of the sky. The Secret Service managed to trace the identity of the dead assassin, and because he was a recluse inventor with no special reason to go after Johnson, also managed to keep the lid on the story.

Not long after Jimmy Carter was in office, he signed a blanket amnesty order, forgiving offenses against young men who had avoided conscription during the Vietnam War years. A deranged ex-Marine sharpshooter made an appearance outside the White House gates during a ceremony on the South Lawn. An agent of the Treasury's I.R.S. investigation unit happened to spot the young man on the street as he hoisted what appeared to be a pool-cue carrying-bag through the gate bars in the general direction of President Carter. Again, the incident went unnoticed by the public.

Winship thought for several moments about the Carter incident, reflecting on the irony of Carter's would-be assassin being an ex-Marine sharpshooter. Kennedy's assassin was an ex-Marine sharpshooter.

Winship stood in the bank of floor-to-ceiling windows of his office, directly behind his desk, the windows looking over toward the White House.

"This new President," he said aloud, though he was alone in the office. "I wonder how long before he's attacked?"

He shook his head, clasped his hands behind his back and paced.

"It wasn't a week before they went after Bush," he said, as if trying to help his thinking by verbalizing the incident.

He stopped in his tracks. "The Mannlicher-Carcaño!" he said. "My God!"

Winship returned to his desk and dropped heavily into his chair. He shuddered. He wiped his forehead with a handkerchief and opened the Slayton dossier.

For the next twenty minutes, Winship read intently, occasionally issuing a favorable grunt as he came across entries such as Slayton's military career as a fighter-bomber, his strong linguistic abilities, his expertise in Oriental martial arts and now the newest episode of his career as a T-Man—the discovery and defusing of a bomb timed to detonate sometime during the arrival of Vice President Bush to a London reception party, the act of a cool and thorough professional.

Cool and professional despite certain drawbacks in his character, Winship thought. He recollected the first time he met Benjamin Justin Slayton.

It was three years ago, when Slayton was a rookie with the Treasury Department, just nicely past his academy training, and assigned to the Bureau of Foreign Asset Control. Hamilton Winship made an inspection tour of the B.F.A.C. one afternoon and was horrified by the sight of one of his T-men, namely, Ben Slayton, and his hair.

"What's your name, son?" Winship asked after a starchy march to Slayton's desk, covered with a clutter of papers and sandwich wrappers.

"Slayton. Benjamin J. And you?"

Winship didn't identify himself. "I would have thought you were lead guitarist for the Rolling Stones," he said instead.

"Indeed I was," Slayton replied, "before I found peace and contentment rummaging through bank balances of sheiks and assorted pals of David Rockefeller temporarily between *coups d'état.*"

"We have an image to maintain here, son, and that means a clean-cut image," Winship thundered.

"Don't sweat the chickenshit, sir, with all due respect. I have on my desk at this moment the certified thievery of one Mohammed Reza Pahlevi, better known as the Shah of Iran, and I can't help but notice that the major banks of the good old U.S. of A. are only too happy to handle his extortion accounts. Now, this outfit I work for has two ways to handle something that's sure to come to a nasty head: refuse to be the Shah's accomplice in the looting of Iran, or make a big fuss about the length of my hair."

Winship's jowls trembled and quaked. Young Slayton regarded him with an expression that betrayed not a whit of emotion. Slayton had no way of knowing that Winship agreed with him, and Winship, at that time, had no way of knowing the destiny of their relationship. Besides, Winship had a role to play.

"Cut your hair," Winship said. "That's an order. And

that's all." He turned on his heel and walked away, red-faced.

The next day, he received a memorandum from Ben Slayton which read, "Hair has been duly trimmed. However, I stand by my remarks."

Winship did not reply to the brash young agent. But he quietly admired him.

Now he was in receipt of another Slayton memorandum, which he read for the fourth time. For the fourth time, he was struck by the last line:

". . . I don't mind losing it all for Georgie, or even Ronnie, for that matter; but I would greatly appreciate in the future knowing when I am to be a decoy."

Winship permitted himself a small laugh.

Earlier in the memo, Slayton had suggested a confidential meeting. It was this request that had occupied Winship's thoughts today, this request that had prompted his historical remembrances, this request that had revived his terrible, unshakeable belief that certain ugly events had a grim connection.

Benjamin Justin Slayton, whose life was spread before Winship on paper, had stepped into the shadows of a nightmare. Did Slayton know where he was treading?

Winship knew only that there was no time to waste in finding out about this Slayton fellow. He telephoned his wife.

"Edith," he said to her, "I want you to arrange a party. Purely a social thing. Mix it up. You know, some serious types and some frivolous. Maybe a bit of the press as well.

"I should like to watch a certain young man."

Nine

"I don't suppose you're able to break it?"

The woman's words came in short gasps, plaintively. She rolled out of Ben Slayton's arms to the edge of her side of the bed and pouted. Slayton moved to her.

"Ben? Oh why?"

"Sorry, love. Command appearance."

He put an arm around her, found her soft and yielding, turned her toward him. He kissed her, gently and properly, and she responded with an involuntary shudder that began in her shoulders and worked itself down to her loins.

Slayton drew her tightly to his body. Her breasts pressed hard against his chest. Their hips swayed together, in a slow, undulating rhythm as they continued their embrace.

Her face was flushed and warm, expectant. He kissed her eyes and her chin. She brushed her long fingers over his taut skin. A fire was building.

"Let me ride you," she said, leaning over his face now, kissing him languorously on the chest and forehead, on his shoulders. "Let me try to keep you to myself."

She straddled his hips as he lay flat on his back, lowering herself to meet his manhood. He moaned, with a touch of helplessness in his voice that pleased her. She bent her head and kissed his lips.

He dug his fingers into the soft flesh of her round hips, guiding her downward, rocking her. Her breasts bobbled not far from his face. She used one hand to pull his head to her bosom.

He tasted the sweetness of her skin, the different textures of soft breast and rigid nipples; and he listened as she cried out each time she thrust herself down on him, again and again, going on long after he had spent himself inside her.

Now dizzy and pleasantly exhausted, they lay on the bed's cool linens, their naked bodies covered only by a sheet and a thin blanket.

Slayton watched the sun rising over the treeline in the east. Bare wooden limbs were tinged with a cold orange. The day would dawn bright and chill.

She clung to him, like a small child. He could smell her crisp scent, gentle and feminine, and the feral odors of their love-making. Women, he thought; such gentle creatures, capable of such frequent and unbridled passion, truly deadlier than the male.

When his breathing returned to normal, he leaned across her lush body for the nightstand, brushing the sheet and blanket away from her breasts. He kissed her breasts and they grew instantly rigid at the tips.

But he ignored this second chance, reaching instead for the nightstand. He slid open a small drawer, felt for the box he knew to be there.

"A token of our time together," he said, holding out the box to her.

Slayton had met her several months ago at the Kennedy Center, during a performance of *Evita*. She was with another man and Slayton was with another woman. But accessories didn't matter. Slayton smiled at her during intermission while the two waited for their respective partners to return from the *pissoirs*.

He had said, "We'll have lunch tomorrow."

And she had sputtered something about a trial beginning tomorrow, how she was a lawyer and how this was a major case—

"Break the date," he told her.

She did, and they dined that next afternoon. And evening. And at breakfast the next morning, in her apartment.

She looked so much like Jean Marie . . . he thought it

68

then and he thought it now, as she examined the contents of the box, holding it up to the morning light shafting in through the windows.

"A sapphire," she said. "A perfect star sapphire. It's beautiful, Ben. Gorgeous."

Then she pouted, jutting out her lower lip, which was about twice the fullness of her upper number. The Julie Christie look.

"I'd rather have you, especially today," she said.

"So you shall, my flower. But not today. The sapphire will have to do until I return. Take care of things."

But he made no effort then to leave the bed. Instead, he lay back, as if to enjoy a cigarette, had he been a smoking man. She hugged him, nodding her acceptance, silently understanding.

Slayton was momentarily saddened. Then he snapped out of it. He understood the meaning of Winship's invitation and knew he had to attend. It was the Washington way.

He closed his eyes, pretending to sleep, listening until his woman drifted off for another hour or two of sleep before rising for the day. Only then did Slayton slip out of the bed.

Quietly, he showered and dressed in jeans, boots, and an oiled wool sweater. He made coffee, and downed two cups while he watered vegetables and flower plants in the greenhouse at the far end of the kitchen.

The greenhouse was an adjunct of the solar heating unit Slayton had constructed on the south side of his house. He had first seen this combination in Vietnam, in the rural cities and villages outside Saigon—or Ho Chi Minh City. Slayton had immediately admired the self-sufficiency of the Vietnamese people and determined to build a home of his own modeled after the typical Vietnamese plan. Even the poorest home was rigged with a solar heat and power generator; even the poorest home contained its own greenhouse.

Jean Marie had loved this greenhouse.

Slayton had met her in his stock car racing days, an improbable but thoroughly enjoyable time of his life, a necessary bridge between his discharge from the Air Force, the resumption of his scholastic life at the University of Michigan, his days of political activism as a member of the Vietnam Veterans Against the War, and his life today as a T-man.

Jean Marie Parrish had come to the races that day in a tank town outside Washington, a town on the circuit Ben Slayton rode in. He remembered everything they talked about, but only a few things about their actual meeting.

He was driving a '72 Pontiac LeMans turbo-charger in those days, and he was winning a good percentage of the events he entered. The day he met Jean Marie was his biggest payday yet.

It was a perfect Indian Summer Saturday. A high school band played the national anthem as all the drivers, in toggle suits with helmets held respectfully over the heart, stared at the flag flapping in the breeze. The dull roar of racing engines and the pervasive smell of motor oil accompanied the ritual music.

Slayton, as usual, was doing stomach exercises while he stood waiting to race, a practice which he found calmed him. He forced his stomach out, then sucked it in, out, then in. . . .

He heard a woman's laughter and turned around. He could have reached out and touched her. She sat in a private box behind him. Or rather stood, her hand across her heart as the band played on. She wasn't singing the words to the national anthem; she watched Ben Slayton's stomach making its peculiar motions and she found it funny.

Embarrassed and angry at the same time, Slayton quickly turned away from her, but not quickly enough to erase the image of her face from his mind.

She was dark-skinned from the sun. Her hair was titian, her eyes a very dark blue, large and wide-set on her face. Her mouth was generous, her nose delicate. She had an intelligent and joyous look. In her face, he saw his future. Never had a woman had such an affect on him, such an all-encompassing, powerful effect.

The band's contribution to the day of racing and gambling was blessedly over. Slayton had never quite understood why the national anthem always had to be played for races and side bets.

He took the wheel of his LeMans, and his seconds strapped him in. His gloved hands gave a final check to the

70

roll bar, he revved the engine some to check for the bounce of the tachometer needle, and, without thinking, glanced back at the stands, to the box where the laughing woman had been. He saw her watching him. When their eyes made contact, she waved to him.

A final check of the mirrors while he heard the starter's count-down. He kept his eyes peeled on the track, depending on his ears to hear the gun fire above the cacophony of engine noise and on his peripheral vision for the downsweep of black-and-white checkered flag.

He nudged the accelerator with his right foot, and made the LeMans jump from the line. He had enough play left to jump his car out in front of his competitors once he had left the line.

Slayton was an excellent racer. With his fourteen- or fifteen-inch starting advantage, he nosed the car inward, toward the close track. He had the edge over cars whose drivers drew the favored positions. He forced one and then another driver to take his dust as he steered relentlessly for the inside track.

Slayton had reached better than one hundred miles an hour in twelve seconds, a credit to his father's excellent teaching, he thought, as he eyed the instrument panel. More power was needed as he went into the turn, he noticed, or else he would hit the wall.

He gritted his teeth, and the muscles in his arms tensed as he held the wheel in a perfect straight line, making sure the wheels were in a square. Then he punched down hard on the accelerator, delivering a sudden burst of torque to the power train. The LeMans held the track as if it were glued to the pavement. Slowly, Slayton inched the wheel into the turn, minimizing the dangerous friction that could flip the fast-moving vehicle.

Fully half a length in front of the only car threatening his victory, Slayton took the chance of torquing into a bank turn. For a suspended second, he thought he might lose control. The vibration was terribly strong, sweat streamed off his face, his arms, and his hands. But he held on, turning, turning . . . and he imagined that he heard the laughing woman, the beautiful laughing woman.

71

He felt the tremendous rush of free air as he zoomed past his competitor, to the clear command of the track. Gently, Slayton worked the LeMans up into the safety of the oval bank. No one would catch him now. He punched the accelerator . . . one hundred and twenty, one hundred and thirty, one hundred and forty-eight miles per hour. Then he topped one-fifty, leaving more than a dozen lengths of space between his LeMans and what would be the second-place driver.

At the end, he climbed out of his car more wobble-legged than he had ever remembered. It had been a grueling race, one in which he had had to battle for all the concentration he could muster, for he had wanted to think only of the face of the laughing woman.

He had set a record that day, he learned as fellow drivers and racing association officials pummeled him on his back and shouted their congratulations. Slayton was floating somewhere above the praise, his perspiration-blinded eyes searching the stands for the vision of that titian-haired woman who had laughed at his stomach exercises.

He took a few unconscious steps in a remembered direction, and suddenly saw her. She waved to him with unrestrained enthusiasm. He ran toward her. She leaned out of her box and nearly fell to the tarmac. A man caught her just in time—her father, as it happened.

Slayton could say nothing. She shouted something like congratulations to him. Dazed and smiling, he moved as close to her as the confines of her spectator's box would allow. She pecked his damp cheek. And then he found his voice.

"Wait here," he said. "I'd like to meet you after."

"Well, the boy speaks!" the older man with her remarked.

"I'll be here," she promised.

And she was.

It was an awkward first hour. Slayton found it difficult to lurch into conversation with Jean Marie, though with her father the talk was a breeze. He was a race fan, and Slayton found himself discoursing on the finer points of racing cams and splinter carbs, all of which the woman he loved found less than enthralling.

But finally her father left, a private sort of laughter trailing behind him as he walked away, and Ben and Jean were alone. He began compulsively telling her about himself, as if there was not a moment to lose.

. . . Did he know even then, that first time he spoke with her?

He told her of his wartime experiences, how he had grown sick and ashamed of the profiteering he saw all about him, by the immorality of the war itself, by the tragedy he could see that the war would bring to the lives of its veterans; he told her about his father, a police captain in Ann Arbor who had died of a heart attack while he was somewhere over Vietnam dropping a payload of destruction in the name of democracy, how he had loved the man, how they had built an impressive collection of Hudson automobiles and vintage Packards and Cadillacs. He told her how his prize possession was an ivory 1952 Nash-Healey two-seater designed by Pinin Farina; how he had joined the Vietnam Veterans Against the War when he returned home to Michigan, then dropped out when he realized that his radical friends seemed to have no vision beyond their next television appearance; how he had amassed a huge collection of literate mystery novels during the time he studied langauge, diplomacy, and politics at the University of Michigan.

She told him less about herself. But enough. She was a serious student of music, a substitute flautist with the National Symphony in Washington, a College of William and Mary fine arts major, and the grateful beneficiary of a rich father.

The two of them were inseparable from that first meeting. Within sixty days, they were married. Again, it seemed to Slayton that there was no time to lose.

Jean Marie's father presented the pair with the gift of fifty acres of rolling woods and field near Mount Vernon —ancestral land. He had enjoyed hearing Ben's talk of building a self-sufficient home on acreage somewhere outside Washington, where he was seeking federal law enforcement work with the help of a Michigan Congressman who had been a friend of his late father.

There could have been no happier couple.

Slayton built on the land his father-in-law had given them.

The house was first to go up, a large, rambling affair built of logs and stone and surrounded by verandas and decks. The south side was entirely glass, a system of solar heating panels over the greenhouse.

He built a windmill and managed to generate nearly one-third of his own electricity. Then he added a hangar, to house a single-engine Cessna he had managed to win in a poker game in Thailand. Adjacent to the hangar, he built a sixteen-stall garage for his cars.

Jean Marie worked on arranging a gourmet kitchen for the house, saw to the growing of herbs and spices, vegetables, and even a few citrus plants in the greenhouse, and set off a generous part of the house for Ben's library, to which her father added a considerable number of rare leather-bound editions, oak floor-to-ceiling bookshelves to line the room, a pair of Persian rugs, and a ceiling of embossed goat skin.

Slayton won appointment to the Treasury Department as a provisional agent, subject to his successfully completing the academy training. On the eve of his graduation day, Slayton received word from Michigan that his mother had died.

. . . *Time is all we have.*

The thought reverberated in his head as he attended the funeral, his wife at his side. She became overwhelmingly precious to him.

When they returned to Virginia, Jean Marie's father had one further lavish gift for the couple, a gift requiring a great deal of Ben's increasingly valuable time. Between the work on the "farm," as he and Jean called their place, and his work in Washington for Treasury, Slayton was a very active man. But Jean's father insisted. The two were to sit for an oil portrait. And sit they did.

Ten days after the portrait was hung above the library fireplace, Jean Marie died in her sleep.

"I wanted to tell you all along," her father told Ben as the two men drank together through the first shattering night of grief, "but Jean made me keep it to myself.

"She's been sick a long time, Ben, since when she was a girl. It meant there were a lot of things she couldn't have, a lot of times she couldn't share with other girls her age. She met you and she fell in love and she wanted the time to-gether, however brief it would be. I wouldn't deny her that wish, or endanger it, by telling you."

The older man finished his brandy and then looked at his son-in-law with a nearly helpless plea in his eyes.

"You understand, Ben?"

He did. "I wanted the time, too. I could have known."

Now, alone in the surroundings that he and Jean Marie had created, he would be reminded of her always. It had been a good time in his life, providing him strong memories with which to go forward.

He found progress in his life, in his work. Slayton had compiled an impressive record of achievement at Treasury, a record that could not be denied him in spite of his occasional contentiousness. He had been good at whatever he had done, in whatever division he served. He would be noticed by someone, at some time.

Slayton believed himself not simply slated for career promotion; he believed himself at a strange and exciting starting point of a new life. He knew he was uniquely fit, by qualification and circumstance. He had been strengthened by love and support in his past, so much so that he understood the power of his complete personal freedom for the future. He was ready and capable of making a blind leap into the dark.

He was neither humbled nor mystified by his fateful conclusion. Slayton merely deduced. He had been waiting for the time, ever since first meeting Hamilton Winship. That early impression, the impression of a man biding his time in a role, had reminded Slayton of a piece of dialogue from R. Wright Campbell's finely textured novel of political intrigue, *The Spy Who Sat and Waited:*

". . . 'I will survive. You see, I am a patient man and easily overlooked.' "

Slayton's own discreet investigation of Winship had only strengthened initial impressions. And tonight, by the ritual of the Washington party, the two men would perform for one another; they would test one another; they would seal some desperate destiny.

Ten

WASHINGTON, D.C., 9 p.m. St. Valentine's Day, 1981

Slayton eased the Nash-Healey around the tight corner leading off the avenue to the Winship residence in Washington's exclusive Georgetown district.

He had been chilly the entire twelve-mile trip in from Mount Vernon, despite the wheezing of the tiny gasoline-powered heater below the dashboard. It was, Slayton reasoned, quaking with the cold in the tiny canvas-topped passenger compartment, a small price to pay, this discomfort. The car was an absolute classic, as underappreciated as it was even in its day.

The Nash-Healey was one of the few true sports cars made in the United States, the happy attempt by the late Nash Corporation to spruce up its line. Even the most biased Nash executive had to know that the Nash selection resembled a display of bathtubs more than an array of fine cars.

So in 1952, the Italian designer Pinan Farina was brought to Detroit to rescue the Nash. And what a job he did of it.

Slayton's was one of the very first Nash-Healeys off the factory assembly line. It had a sleek ivory body, sloped downward at the front of its long hood, was notched with tiny tailfins in back. An oval chrome grille with hooded headlights, the sparest of chrome bumpers fore and aft, and balloon tires set around gleaming convex hub caps gave the ship its European dash.

Under the protracted hood was a powerful, mostly aluminum-cast six-cylinder V-block engine, quite a forward-looking plant in its day. It still ran like a dream. In the dry months of October and November, Slayton would run the Nash-Healey full-out, and the machine would respond as if it were a greyhound dog aching for the relief of a race track.

The engine purred as Slayton wheeled the car to the curb front outside the Winship home. A liveried black man opened the door for him and announced that he was to park the guests' cars. Slayton tried to give him a pair of dollar bills for his trouble.

"No way," the porter said. "This is a privilege. Can this be a Nash-Healey?"

"The very one," Slayton answered. There was a bond between the men. Few could identify the car properly. Only the most discriminating.

"A rare beauty," the porter said.

"And a rare night."

Slayton turned and walked to the front stoop of Winship's house, an ivy-covered red brick townhouse at mid-block with a fine green-and-gold Georgian door.

A butler took his coat and gloves, and before he was spotted by his hosts, Slayton had a chance to take in the scene.

It was a typical Georgetown gathering, minus only the posturing of Presidential Cabinet and sub-Cabinet appointees, as it was too early in the new regime for that sort of thing. Slayton missed most especially the antics of Hamilton Jordan from the Carter administration. He had been in a home much like the one he now stood in when Jordan, it had been rumored and fiercely denied by Hamilton the next day, ogled the decolletage of the Egyptian ambassador's wife and remarked, "I do believe I see the great pyramids."

The Congressional representation was mostly Democratic, reflecting the Winships' personal political affiliations, though a few Republican curiosities were milling about. Slayton couldn't take his eyes off Alfonse D'Amato, the new Senator from New York. He was trying to decide the merits of a description of D'Amato he had heard somewhere, that the Senator closely resembled a ferret.

Diplomats were in great abundance, of course. The biggest delegation were elegant Third Worlders whose capitals couldn't provide food and drink that matched the quality and quantity of that offered at the simplest American diner. Often this bunch was purely hungry, Slayton had learned.

The women were uniformly horselike. The doughy matrons who had by some mysterious means laid claim to their husbands decades earlier and were now resting on their plump laurels, content to allow the menfolk their cheap distractions while they quietly kept the books.

The exception, Slayton quickly saw, was the wife of the French ambassador, a Monsieur LaRoque. LaRoque had recently married a twenty-seven-year-old star of the French cinema, known in Paris simply as Adrienne. LaRoque himself was an aging debauchee. The flesh sagged off his face like a cake that had been left out in the rain. The only icing was a little Hitleresque mustache. His eyes were tired, as if he'd been up all night before sweating it out with a pair of fourteen-year-old boys.

LaRoque's wife, on the other hand, was a wondrously beautiful creature. It was as if this couple were the gender opposites of Senator John Warner and his new wife, the corpulent Elizabeth Taylor, both of whom were standing nearby the LaRoques.

Adrienne LaRoque was a tall and graceful woman, perhaps four inches taller than her squat husband; she had dark brown hair and almond-colored eyes; and a voice that Slayton cocked his ear to hear, a familiar husky-feminine voice. He had seen one of her films and had been reminded, though she looked nothing like her, of Lauren Bacall in her early days.

Slayton began moving toward the LaRoques. Senator Warner and Elizabeth Taylor waved to him, signaling him to join their circle, thinking he had seen their gesture.

He was stopped by Edith Winship.

"So, you must be Benjamin Justin Slayton," she said.

"The same." He took her hand and kissed it in the continental manner. She blushed—slightly, girlishly. He liked her immediately.

"Hamilton pointed you out to me when you entered," she explained. She pointed now across the room, to her husband, who tipped his glass toward them. He was busy speaking to Jim Brady, the President's press secretary.

"Come and I'll introduce you to whoever you may not know," she said, draping her arm in his.

"The French ambassador," Slayton said. "I've never had the pleasure."

Edith Winship arched her brows at this and whispered to Slayton, "Pity that old goat has the pleasure. My guess is that you'd know how better to use it."

They reached the LaRoques. Slayton extended his hand in greeting to LaRoque, but didn't look at him. He and Adrienne locked gazes.

"I'll leave you all now," Edith Winship said, fluttering off toward the Warners. Elizabeth Taylor looked miffed.

LaRoque muttered something, and continued a conversation with a man to his right, an Austrian who looked every bit as debauched and as wearied by it as LaRoque.

"Shall we have a moment's time together?" Slayton asked Adrienne.

"Of course," she said.

All eyes in the room followed the handsome couple as they glided toward a bar and helped themselves to champagne.

They talked for ten minutes. Adrienne favored him with a few bits of Parisian film gossip, indicated her boredom for Washington and most things American, and said she wished she were home in France, basking in the warm sun of Nice. Slayton imagined himself in bed with her, with her long legs wrapped around his back.

She noticed that he wasn't listening to her words. She smiled and covered his hand with hers.

"I can read your thoughts," she said, her voice heavy with its French accent. "Can you read mine?"

"I believe I can. You just thought, 'Yes, I'd love to have a private drink with this man.'"

"Then let's go," she said, "but not far."

Slayton looked around the room. The only escape was a stairway. She watched him look at it.

"I'll go up, to the powder room. You follow in a few minutes. We'll meet somewhere up there."

It was just as she said. When Slayton made his way up the stairs, he heard her whisper, from a doorway off the corridor.

He entered a large bedroom, tastefully furnished and equipped, as most of Georgetown's elegant homes were, with a small fireplace.

"Now, we're alone," she said, smiling, somewhat shyly.

Slayton took her shoulders in his hands and pulled her toward him. She did not resist.

They moved together quickly, hungrily, embracing with parted lips. Slayton slipped his fingers beneath the wispy strands of her gown and pulled the top slowly over her breasts, baring them.

He held her breasts in his hands, then leaned down to kiss them. Adrienne locked her fingers behind his head, urging him on, then urging him downward.

Slayton dropped his hands to her hips and grasped the lower portion of her gown, raised it up over her knees, then her smooth thighs, to her waist. She was naked beneath the gown.

He caressed her gently, wetting her, causing her to tremble and growl something wicked in French. Then he rose to face her. He could see the helplessness in her face. She was his.

She bent to undo his trousers, pleasuring him with her touch and her taste. Slayton steadied himself as she worked on him, playfully, expertly.

When she had tired, Slayton guided her to the edge of a canopied bed. Standing at the side, Slayton lifted her right leg at the knee, propping it up on the bed. He stood behind her, raised her gown and moved in close.

Behind them, at the door, they heard the sound of a throat clearing itself.

It was Hamilton Winship, wearing an expression of simultaneous disapproval and mischievous envy.

Adrienne let out a small scream that sounded like an

injured forest animal. She pulled furiously at her gown, smoothing it down over her bared buttocks. Her face was very red and her breathing was that of a drowning victim.

She gave Slayton a vicious stare and walked quickly away from him. Her heel caught on an edge of a rug, and she nearly fell flat on her face. Winship caught her and struggled with her, finally righting the lady.

"I am sorry," she said, stiffly.

"But it's Valentine's Day," Winship said, chortling at his own joke.

Slayton calmly zipped up his trousers and straightened his coat and tie. A rare night indeed, he thought.

"Now, my boy," Winship said, approaching Slayton, "I've been meaning to speak to you tonight." He ignored the little assignation he had just witnessed. Interrupted, to be exact.

"Come with me."

Slayton followed Winship's lead, down the opposite end of the second-floor corridor to a back stairway. The two men clattered down the bare wood steps. At the bottom, a door led into the kitchen, where a chef and his charges were about to serve the evening buffet as soon as they stopped throwing knives at one another. A second door led to Winship's study.

It was a dark and heavy room, though it could be much lighter during the day, Slayton could see, with a pair of large glass doors leading out into the garden area of the house. Slayton examined the paintings, grouped above yet another fireplace in the Winship household.

Slayton was invited to rest in the striped Regency chair, one of two at either side of Winship's burnished teakwood desk. Winship flicked on the Tiffany lamp at the edge of his desk.

"The Marthés," Slayton said, "are excellent. I wish I had one myself."

Winship smiled. He looked toward the painting unconsciously when Slayton mentioned it.

"You are an art fancier, Mr. Slayton?"

"I fancy anything artful, Mr. Winship."

"Have you any idea why you're here?"

"Of course."

Winship studied the young man in front of him. They were of two completely different generations, two completely different social worlds. And yet they saw something of each other in their opposites.

"This is not simply to clear up any questions you may have about the Bush incident."

"No sir, I expect not," Slayton said. "I would guess you wish to discuss Hurgett and Samuels."

"Do you believe their deaths are related?"

"Of course. Don't you?"

Winship was pleasantly stunned.

"What do you know about me?" he asked Slayton.

"I know that your instincts are right. I know you are one of the very few in command of the intelligence network who understands the danger of outlaws in our midst, outlaws of our own making. I know that you're unable to do anything about it. Just now, that is."

"You know a great deal more than most young agents."

"Elementary, my dear Winship."

The two men laughed. Winship got up from his chair and served brandy from a sideboard.

"What makes you believe that the Hurgett and Samuels deaths are related?" Winship asked.

"Both were assassinations. Different styles. The first was a textbook clean shot job. The second was most probably a matter of nicotine poisoning."

Winship formed a question mark with his eyebrows.

"Samuels had a history of heart trouble, I seem to recall. If you were to give me a few cigarettes—better yet, cigars— I could extract enough pure nicotine through a heating and simple distillation process to kill a man like that with a few drops in his food or coffee."

"But the autopsy?" Winship asked.

"First of all, I assume there was none. Second, an autopsy in no way guarantees that a chemical cause of death will be determined.

"Most autopsies are *pro forma*. Even traceable poisons are not traced unless there is reason to suspect foul play, which, in Samuels' case, there was not. Unless the forensic pathologist is on his toes and suspicious, a poison of the colloidal family that would simulate the symptoms of heart failure would be virtually untraceable. You'd be home safe using extracted nicotine, for example."

"And how do you come by this knowledge, Slayton?"

"Perhaps in the same manner you did. And like you, sir, I would respectfully decline to reveal my sources."

"A respectful and respectable answer. I like you, Slayton. Tell me something of your beliefs in the purposes of intelligence work."

Slayton sat back in his chair and took a deep breath.

"Properly conducted intelligence can prevent the sort of geopolitical incompetence we saw in the Carter administration, not to mention historical ignorance. Improperly conducted intelligence work reminds me of the pious humanitarian described by Emerson: 'We mean well and do ill, and then justify our ill-doing by our well-meaning.' "

Winship beamed.

"It's probably vital in either case," Slayton added. "After all, the world isn't run by the League of Women Voters."

"Yes, I like you very much, Slayton."

Winship slid open the center top drawer of his desk. He removed a box and folded his hands over it while he spoke.

"Now, we've had two members of Congress slain in Europe in the past few months. Both assassinated, as you correctly note."

Slayton sipped his brandy. The excitement inside him was growing.

"In the case of Hurgett, a Mannlicher-Carcaño was the weapon—"

"The same rifle that killed Kennedy. President Kennedy."

"Yes. . . and you're absolutely right about the nicotine poisoning."

"Then the death of Samuels—"

"Yes. Colloidal family poisoning. Methods known only to those with connections to either C.I.A., K.G.B. or Mossad. We can rule out the K.G.B. and Mossad, I should think."

"Is there something that has been held back from public

knowledge in these cases, as in the attempt against Bush?"

"You are most perceptive, once again, Slayton."

"Thank you."

"Not at all. Here, look at these."

Winship spilled the contents of the box he held, a rolled-up cylinder of paper retrieved from the spent shell of the Mannlicher-Carcaño, the telegram from Italy delivered to Samuels' widow. The message in each case, *"Non, Je Ne Regrette Rien."*

"It's from Piaf," Slayton said, looking up.

"Yes, her theme song," Winship said.

" 'I regret nothing.' "

Winship watched for signs of Slayton's realization of the meaning of these clues.

Slayton asked, "Vice President Bush would have been the third victim in this spree?"

"That is one of the mysteries you are assigned to solve," Winship said. "The other, of course, is who, exactly, stands behind this terrorism."

The hint of understanding showed finally in Slayton's eyes. Winship read it.

Slayton's throat was dry as he said, "The man who escaped Sidi bel Abbès?"

"Very possibly." Winship's voice was low. The two men completely understood one another. They were allied. "He strongly resembles the magnified photographs of an unidentified man in Dealey Plaza in Dallas, November 22, 1963."

Winship let this sink into the sensibilities of the young man seated at his desk.

"What is he trying—"

"That is precisely what I want to have you first find out and then halt, by whatever means necessary. Do you understand, Slayton?"

"I understand the real world."

"Yes . . . and so do I. You are from this moment on assigned to report to no one but me. I want you to understand the importance of your mission. These two assassinations were warnings. And the Bush matter was almost the same. President Reagan will be the next target."

Slayton nodded mutely.

"The planning is underway at the White House for a trip by the President to Tokyo. I must assume that word of this scheduling work has reached the C.I.A., and is therefore known to everyone in the terrorist underground by now.

"I believe that he is out there now, planning the assassination of President Reagan."

"He?"

Winship stood up. He replaced the papers with the Piaf song titles in the box, which he slid back into his desk. Before answering, he walked to the fireplace.

"You know who I'm talking about," Winship said.

"Yes," Slayton said. "The Wolf."

"Can you be prepared to leave in the morning?"

"Yes."

PART TWO

Eleven

ANDORRA, the Pyrenees, 15 March 1981

He had been in the mountain city-state for a month, one more lone figure mingling easily with the drifting current of travelers who passed the tiny principality situated between France and Spain.

It was an odd little nation, transformed in only two decades from a place of bucolic poverty to fabulous wealth, much of it amassed by suspicious means. It was the only place in the Pyrenees that one might find a traffic jam surrounding a bazaar, the only place in the world where real estate value is measured by the palm of the hand, a choice "square palm" in the capital fetching up to $85.

Side by side with men of enormous fortune who spend millions of Spanish pesetas and French francs to sustain their compulsive privacies are the flotsam of the anarchist spirit of the 1960s, American and European men and women in advanced states of adolescence despite their mid-thirties ages.

For both the questionably rich and the aimless, Andorra is a convenient way station, a way of life in which few ask questions of themselves or others.

Andorra's duty-free and virtually law-free status is a magnet to disparate sorts. Nothing is illegal, therefore everything is legal. Smuggling through Andorra's narrow, rugged mountain passes is an old-fashioned enterprise, requiring strong bodies and nimble minds, skilled capital and highly skilled labor. And little sense of the curious.

Seven unregulated and highly secretive Andorran banks do a very brisk business of laundering Spanish pesetas moving toward Switzerland, and northern European currencies on their way to the Bahamas. There is no penal code, no land register, no customs service, and no regulations governing banks or foreign-owned companies. Those visitors unwise enough to commit anything so boorish as a felony are collared by someone from the forty-five-man police force and shipped off to a nearby town in France or Spain for cooling.

The capital, which carries the name Andorra as well, thoughtfully provides a small slum in the old Catalan district, far removed from the great avenues of shops featuring high-quality electronics at prices thirty percent lower —or more—than legal retail rates in Paris or Madrid, Chivas Regal at prices below wholesale, French cheeses, more Mary Quant cosmetics than France and Switzerland combined would have available, and an embarrassment of Nikons and Sonys.

In this slum, which in some other city would pass as a slightly gamey, somewhat down-at-the-heels working-class quarter, he had roomed for a month on the top floor of a four-story boarding house. Like others before him and those to follow, he had simply appeared one day in the street asking for a room, a cheap restaurant, and where he might possibly find a bit of work.

In a few days, he was crating up color television sets, making sure they would survive the rigors of the smuggling routes southward into Spain, where the border could be bought from the guards.

A Barcelona entrepreneur offered the American stranger two hundred pesetas per hour to start, and he had enjoyed the look of pleasant surprise in the American's face until the man in need of the job calculated the wage at less than three dollars. When the television sets would reach their destination, on the backs of the wily smuggler soldiers, customers would be assessed on the poundage basis, currently seven dollars per pound, or about $175 for a television set—a peerless bargain for the consumer and a whopping profit for the Barcelona entrepreneur.

Today he had worked a full nine hours, beginning at dawn. The Spaniard had given him the next day off and a thousand-peseta bonus for diligence. He was drinking some of it in his neighborhood saloon.

His attention was drawn to a tallish blonde woman who sauntered into the bar, dressed all in denim save for a pair of Frye boots that looked rather new and a yellow cotton shirt with a green palm tree embroidered just above her left breast, which, like its mate, was unrestricted by a brassiere.

She wore colored glasses of a violet tint, the kind that gave mystique rather than eye shade. Her hair was thick and clean and hung straight as a Dutch boy's. Her narrow hips were boyish as well. He guessed her age at thirty-seven.

The barman shuffled toward her and nodded in recognition. She said something he couldn't hear clearly. The barman drew a draught of ale and accepted francs in payment.

He had not seen her in the month he had been coming into the saloon, which was maybe four times a week, at quite varied hours. She was astonishingly beautiful, he thought, with an unmistakeable air of intelligence and independence. Was she a whore? He asked this of the barman, whom he had summoned to his end for a refill of his lager and schnapps.

"In this neighborhood?" the barman snorted in fraternal ridicule. "With all that Andorra can offer to a whore? What would such a woman find here with the Catalonians? You make a joke with me."

The barman completed his order and explained about her, leaning closely to the American.

"She is German. Her name is Sigrid. I don't know the rest. All of the men would like to know her, but none have been able. Somewhere in the hills, outside the city, is where she lives. Maybe every other month she comes in here, for an ale or two. And she stares out the window to the street, like she is doing now, watching her car. You see it there?"

He couldn't possibly miss it, nor could anyone else in the scruffy neighborhood. A dark green Maserati was out of place in a street lined with ancient and heavily dented Volks-wagens.

He moved toward her, past the other mumbling men and the few other women at the bar, through the clouds of blue cigarette smoke cut by shafts of setting sunlight. She ignored him, keeping her eyes fastened on her car and on the small knot of neighborhood boys gathered around it.

"A beautiful automobile," he said to her in German, taking a spot at the rail next to her. He was quite close, but she wouldn't turn to him. He said, "I love beautiful cars. And beautiful women."

With this she turned and, expressionless, examined him. Her eyes moved from his head to his feet, disdainfully. She responded to him in English, as if to insult his attempts at her native tongue.

"Who are you?"

"My name is Ben. I'm American, just passing through." She nodded and smiled. It wasn't an unfriendly smile.

"Your name is . . . what?" He had switched to English.

"Sigrid. And you want to buy me a drink?"

"Of course."

"Then you should do it."

The barman was not far away. He had watched the approach with admiration and would have whispered his congratulations if it had been politic to do so. But not with Sigrid about. She was too austere, too absent of assumable humor, too German.

"*Danke*," she said to him, lifting her glass in toast.

They drank. Then Sigrid removed her tinted glasses, revealing large, clear eyes of emerald.

"What did you do before you came to Andorra?" she asked, hurriedly. She didn't wish to talk about herself.

"I was a war criminal."

He had surprised her, as he intended. Her imperious defenses were shattered. Say the words "war criminal" to a German when you have the conversational drop on him—or her—and you can reduce a hun quite quickly.

She was trying to speak, but her words came out in a stammer, a mix of German and French and English, betraying her sudden confusion. He looked at her, at her eyes and

92

the subtle touch of maroon on her wide lips. *Gott im Himmel,* she was beautiful!

"Vietnam," he said to her before she could get sufficiently back in control to speak in sentences of any language. "I was a fighter bomber. It was a terrible time in my life. I suffered while I was there, and longer, years longer, when I returned home. I felt like a criminal. I still do."

Outside, on the street, the boys were moving away from the Maserati, going their separate ways home to supper. Sigrid could relax a bit.

"Can we sit down?" he asked. He waved his hand toward a booth. "It's got a good view of the street, as you can see. Your car will be all right, I'm sure."

Sigrid nodded, and they took the booth. Ben looked back over his shoulder for the barman, to order up more drinks. The barman formed an approving circle with the thumb and forefinger of his right hand. Drinks would be on the way.

"Tell me about it," she said. "I mean about the war in Vietnam."

"I enlisted," he began, "during the early years, thinking I was doing the right thing, making the world safe for democracy and all. Besides, I thought that the air force experience would be useful.

"But then I got sick. Not physically. But sick just the same, knowing I was killing by remote control. All bombers go through the same thing.

"It got to the point where I didn't feel any more. No feeling at all—subhuman. I was an automaton, a deadly robot. I just flew and bombed, flew and bombed. And I waited for the same fate for myself. Someone would get me soon."

Sigrid interrupted. "But did you not believe in your country's leadership?"

"I believed my country had taken leave of its senses. I hoped it would be temporary. I hoped the people of my country would one day remember that . . . remember that . . ."

He looked out the window and scratched his head. If this was the woman he thought she might be, he would have to choose his words carefully.

"Well," he continued, "it must be kept in mind that one man's terrorist is another man's freedom fighter. One must look beyond the easy answers in the press and current history."

"I agree," she said. She leaned forward. He could see the outline of her nipples through her shirt.

"In this case, of course, it was Ho Chi Minh. I didn't think of him at first as the personification. I thought only of the wonder of human survival, the dignity in it. And I thought, 'What odds dignity must always challenge!'

"There I was, piloting a gigantic American bomber, flying in low over peasant villages in the far reaches of a wretched little jungle country. I must have scared the bejeezus out of them all. How many of them had ever even seen a plane close up? Too often. I was raining down death every hour of every day, week after week, month after month.

"And what do you know? A little creature down there called man managed to survive even man's genius for destruction. He managed to survive it because of his defiance, and thank God for defiance. And the one guy down there who shook his fist the strongest was this splindly little slope called Ho Chi Minh. Now there was a courageous man, so courageous he was mystical.

"It was only an accident of birth that I fought against the guy instead of for him."

He stopped to sip his lager, and to let the theatricality of what he had said seep into his suddenly fascinated companion. Some of what he had said he believed. Much of what he said he had let drop around the Catalonian district. Malcontents were always in demand in Andorra, a city which would soon rival Zurich for laissez-faire capitalism and the old fables of Istanbul for international intrigue.

He was happy to see that word had reached Sigrid, as he knew it would reach someone who had to be like her. Some self-styled vanguard.

But would she lead him to the Wolf?

Slayton watched the emerald eyes across the booth glow hot and cold—eyes that contained a passion for razor's edge politics as well as a passionate curiosity about him. He was reminded just how sexy, how completely filled with raw sensuality, were the 1960s.

She smiled for the first time. He had been waiting for this contact for a month. Now he was sure he had made it.

"You have strong principles," she said. Her voice had gone lower. She almost cooed the words. "I like people who are strong. They are survivors. They are the people who should rule."

"They should be together."

Sigrid accepted the gambit.

"Where do you stay?" she asked.

Slayton told her about the rooming house. Then he asked her about her quarters.

"In the mountains," she answered, mystery dripping from her every pore as she looked out into the street. It was nearly dusk now. She turned to him.

"You're an interesting man. Would you like to see where I live?"

He rose from the booth, taking her hand as he stood. Slayton paid the barman, who winked lecherously, and guided Sigrid out the door toward her Maserati.

"I am not just *any* woman," she said, seated behind the wheel. She turned the key in the ignition. The engine responded at once. "You may be surprised."

"I am not just *any* man."

Sigrid smiled at him for the second time.

Then the Maserati rumbled down the narrow slum street to the highway for the long climb into the Pyrenees foothills.

Twelve

WHITE PLAINS, New York, 15 March 1981

He sat at the north end of a long ersatz wooden table in the well-lighted library, close to the government documents section. He looked only slightly older than the high school students on term paper assignments, not out of place at all.

He looked up from the thick paper-bound tomes in front of him. Across the room there were perhaps twenty retirees browsing through the stacks of gothic novels.

From the briefcase on the floor, he produced a yellow legal pad. He pulled a pen out of his pocket after slipping off his trenchcoat.

There was no reason for him to be the least bit nervous, but he looked about the room anyway, his eyes darting from the desk where three flat-chested women did their librarian tasks, to the water fountains where suburban mothers held thirsty snowsuited toddlers, to the steel shelves where he had moments ago found his material, a conveniently canyoned arrangement for amorous teenagers.

No one paid the slightest attention to him.

He wrote the title of the first of two bound documents before him on the top of the first page of his legal pad: *Barrier Penetration Database*. Then as he flipped through the pages of the government book, he noted:

- *First barrier after I make it through the woods, toward*

97

perimeter, will be "barbed tape obstacle." NRC says this will take minimum 15 maximum 21 seconds to clear.

* *If I choose to ram through main security gate with light pick-up, NRC says it would take max 3 seconds, with no damage to truck.*

* *Once at plant itself, approx 300 yards from gate, light explosives necessary to clear 12" reinforced walls; NRC specifies: "Wall is 500 psi concrete with 5/16-inch expanded metal on 2.5" centers. One needs 150 lbs of cutting torch and a 10 lb sledge hammer together with six lbs of bulk explosives to get through in 23 ± 5 minutes."*

* *Roof of nuclear reactor itself is equally vulnerable, according to NRC, to wit: "With 4 lbs of bulk explosive and 20 lb bolt cutters, penetration takes 2.2 ± 0.5 minutes."*

* *Reactor ceiling next. Will need 10 lb bolt cutter, 10 lb sledge hammer and JA-IV Jet-Axe explosive. Entry time, says NRC, 1.6 to 2.4 minutes.*

He spent the next hour making notes, from both the U.S. Government's *Barrier Penetration Database* and a companion study, the three-hundred page *Barrier Technology Handbook*. In addition to careful instructions in the art of surmounting security fences, walls, floors, doors, and windows—skills he already knew as a master—the government books thoughtfully included appendices showing the reader precisely how to slip through corridors undetected and how to scale ladders while carrying the necessary valise full of burglar tools to enter a security installation.

A few weeks earlier, he had been in Washington, where he had dropped into the public reading room of the Nuclear Regulatory Commission. He looked like any other lobbyist, or perhaps like an earnest young man from Ralph Nader's office.

There he read the words of Frank Bevilacqua, vice president of the Combustion Engineering Corporation and a contributor to a 1976 NRC-sponsored workshop at Sandia Laboratories of New Mexico:

"... A small team and possibly even one or two people

with sufficient knowledge and access to the plant equipment can sabotage a sufficient amount of components to cause a release of radioactive material."

A photostat of Bevilacqua's remarks were in his briefcase, along with the industrialist's urgent recommendation:

"Details of plant layout, vital systems, instrumentation and control circuitry and details of vital equipment and plant security systems should not be placed in the public domain."

The young man who had compiled the NRC material also had a satchel full of newspaper clips. Among them was an Associated Press dispatch he had clipped from the October 21, 1979, edition of the Miami *Herald:*

GUARDS CLAIM SECURITY IS LAX AT NUCLEAR POWER PLANT

BUCHANAN, N.Y. (AP)—The men who guard the Indian Point Nuclear Power plant here in upstate New York warn that it is "here for the taking" by skillful terrorists.

Interviewed were several guards, all of whom requested anonymity. They revealed:

• Alarms around the plant were often turned off, and because of heavy traffic the ones turned on sounded so often that "no one pays much attention."

• Fencing around some sections of the installation was so inferior that the Nuclear Regulatory Commission (NRC) made Gleason Security Service, which held the contract for protecting Indian Point, put guards on the spot 24 hours a day.

• Plastic entry cards, used to gain access to the plant's most critical areas, were frequently lost by employees and replaced without question.

A student at nearby Yonkers Community College who last summer held a part-time job as a private guard at Indian Point told the AP, "I still have my ID card."

The student also said training for him and other part-timers like him was "a joke." He said, "Most guards wouldn't know what to do with a gun if they had to use one. Some would blow their foot off first."

The young man's satchel was further full of spiral-bound notebooks containing data he had not bothered to clip in full from newspapers. He would simply come across the information during his normal course of reading newspapers in whatever city he was living at the time.

In this way, he noted that five nuclear power plants across the United States had been shut down in March of '79 due to plumbing inadequacies. "Bad plumbing," he wrote in his notebook, "combined with earthquake activity of even the gentlest measure can cause lethal spillage."

The idea of earthquakes in proximity to nuclear power plants occurred to him because of another jotting dated January 4, 1979:

"Today a gentle quake rolled across Westchester County south of Indian Point. My, my could this be a Biblical foreboding? What a delicious thought.

"Something like 20 million people, or roughly 10% of the American population, live within 50 miles of Indian Point."

One of the young man's notebooks was entirely filled with details of more than two hundred "security incidents," as the NRC called them, most of them recorded by the NRC's predecessor agency, the Atomic Energy Commission. All the incidents occurred between 1967 and 1975, according to the NRC and the AEC, and none mounted had been connected with terrorism.

"However," the young man had noted, "the federal government has either completely ignored or chosen for some reason not to reveal what the press has reported as several hundred pounds of enriched uranium and plutonium that is totally unaccounted for in plant by plant inventories matched against centralized supply records."

Two "security incidents" were boxed with red-ink borders in the young man's notebook. In one case, an incident concerned the matter of a religious fanatic in the Reverend Moon cult who was arrested for selling Moonie "gifts" at the Hanford Atomic Reservation in Washington State and who eluded police and guards for several hours by hiding in a restricted laboratory. That was in June of 1977.

In another case, two antinuclear activists in Virginia had sneaked into a power plant in their state, damaged the fuel rods, and then announced how they had set the stage for dangerous waste leakage, to demonstrate the potential for catastrophic disaster by sabotage. The young activists were convicted of trespassing and jailed.

Further jottings and notations included the words from a 1976 NRC press release:

"No plant has been determined to be out of compliance with existing regulations. All are operating under safeguard plans. Based on our ongoing studies, we perceive no reasonable cause for taking actions beyond the prompt and thoroughgoing ones that have already been initiated."

The young man closed the covers of the two government documents from which he had taken copious notes. He picked up his briefcase and slipped his notebook inside.

As he pulled on his trenchcoat, he thought to himself how overly easy it had been to plot his next course of action.

There had been no special skills involved. No midnight break-ins of the Department of Energy Building in Washington, as he had thought he might have to accomplish when he first arrived in America; no stolen combinations for underground vaults; no hurried snaps of a laser microfilm camera.

He had done these things before, having been trained in his craft since puberty. But nothing in his training had prepared him psychologically for the baffling openness of the American culture, the almost complete lack of concern for the spies swarming all over the country. He wrote it off to the overconfidence of a still young and continental

101

nation, a nation of secure borders unmatched anywhere in the world.

Besides, what had America to fear from the likes of Canada and Mexico?

He shook his head, grinning conspiratorially. What a foolish country, he thought. All his training—training by a man the world would soon bow to—and he had only to drop into a public library, flash a card, and spend all the time he needed with the shelves containing America's secrets.

The young man walked out of the library. It was raining. He stuffed his briefcase into the folds of his trenchcoat to protect it against the weather.

He headed to his car, a ten-year-old Chevrolet, and realized that he now had just about everything he needed to hold the world hostage. Yet he had broken no law.

As he drove off the lot of the White Plains Public Library, he hummed the melody to an advertising air he remembered from his indoctrination period, a full year of being steeped in films and television and books depicting the American popular culture. The tune, he recalled, was sung at the beginning and end of a 1950s television variety show starring Dinah Shore.

"See the U.S.A. in your Chevrolet—America's the greatest land of all!"

And the most naive.

Thirteen

ANDORRA, the Pyrenees, 16 March 1981

They had made love twice before falling asleep. The first time quietly, almost unimaginatively. It was an exploration. The second time was a noisy, sweating affair, wild and abandoned.

As he slept, his half-consciousness reflected on the ride in Sigrid's Maserati up into the hills. Never had he seen such beautiful country, such mysterious hills.

Exposed, heavily eroded granite arched in broken, odd-shaped peaks, moist clouds ringing each formation. Some mad giant, it seemed in his dreams, had flung about great hunks of rock. Some of the rocks landed gracefully, others were heaped haphazardly one atop the other. Inside these formations, soil blown by heavy winds found collection points. Trees rooted themselves precariously from these hidden holes, curling up over the precipices to reach the life-giving rain and sunlight, their haggard limbs resembling at times the legs and arms of human beings.

Mountain peaks clad in these forlorn ranges of trees, half-rooted in granite, disappeared into moonlit fog and heavy clouds. As they drove up the face of the mountain, Ben saw the remains of shacks, once the homes of goat-herders and shepherds, later outlaws who roamed the hills during the some seven hundred years Andorra was fought over by various invasions of French, Spanish, and Moroccans.

Waterfalls, mostly small ones dropping ledge to ledge, connected swiftly moving rivers of ice-cold water. The terrain was hauntingly like that of Dante's inferno.

As they rounded a bend on a heavily rutted, narrow road, near the top of a middle peak, Sigrid had pointed to a massive block of piled stones, huge and black, silhouetted against the backlight of the moon.

"That is where I live," she said. "It is the remains of a castle. The bare remains, I should say."

And so it was.

The castle was little more than a huge round tower, with entrances into underground corridors—or what Slayton assumed were corridors dug into the mountain face— closed by ancient rock slides, probably the result of fierce battle and cannon fire.

There were several floors. Slayton would explore the place in the daylight. His need for the beautiful German woman was sufficiently urgent to keep him in on this clear night. He had followed her across a rotting board that spanned the remains of a moat, then up the narrow steps from the ground floor to Sigrid's loft.

Slits of windows overlooked a wide plain, dropping off more than a thousand feet, Sigrid had told him, to a field of boulders. In the pale yellow illumination of the moon, she had slipped off her clothing, revealing her perfect form.

As he slept now, his mind a jumble of impressions, he shifted in her bed. Momentarily he was confused by the feel of a woman next to him, by the feel of the thin mountain air.

But Slayton's head cleared and he woke fully to her touch. A dull red light was forming in the sky. Soon it would be dawn. Sigrid had already risen and now she was kneeling over his body, her high, soft breasts moving gently to the rhythm of her hands as they massaged his naked chest and stomach.

His eyes were half open as he watched her take hold of his penis. She stroked it softly, a deep gutteral sound cooing in her throat. She leaned downward ⸺⸺ the head of his penis with her lips.

Slayton heard himself rumble, felt himself p⸺ desire as he swelled inside her warm mouth. He l⸺ to her sibilant sounds. He felt her long hair, held h⸺ to him, thrust into her. He could hold back no longer.

When she had finished, she lay back in the bed. He moved to her, covering her chest with his own. As he kissed her, he could taste himself on her lips and tongue.

The two of them twisted into each other, their bodies warm and wet. He was on his back. She slid on top of him, covering the length of his body with her own, her long arms and legs draped over him.

She spread her thighs and sat upright in one quick, smooth motion. Her narrow, taut hips were poised over his erection. She plunged down onto him, filling herself, shouting as she did so.

He watched, transfixed by the sight of his own hard member disappearing into her soft darkness over and over as she moved up and down on him. The sounds of her German words were muffled by the wet sounds of their sex.

Slayton closed his eyes again, weary from the long night and from Sigrid's insatiable passions. He drifted off. He couldn't remember it ending. . . .

. . . When he awakened, it was to the sharp sound of gunfire.

TOKYO, Japan

The apartment house on Ginza Street was quiet. A bell from the nearby square at Tokyo Station signaled the midnight hour. Tomorrow was a work day. The Meijiza and Kabuki Theatres, to the north and south of the apartment house, had long ago dispensed their early evening audiences.

Tokyo is a city of early risers, even in the Ginza, the most fashionable and the most colorful street. Residents of the apartment house were highly paid professionals, for the most part, with a smattering of foreign businessmen assorted diplomats who found it especially convenient because of its proximity to the Imperial Palace and the Diet Building.

Outside, the only sound was that of strolling police officers, dressed in navy blue tunics and red sashes, armed only with nightsticks and whistles. Two blocks away, a mechanized street sweeper could be heard wetting down the pavement, its giant circular brushes rubbing the surface of the street.

The newest tenant in the apartment house glanced out her window to the street. The Ginza was empty, save for the reassuring sight of the police foot patrols. She walked from the window and stubbed out her cigarette in an ashtray full of butts.

Her guests lay quietly sleeping, their bodies strewn about the studio in sleeping bags and beneath blankets spread out on two small sofas and a chair.

She was Italian—of medium size, but much larger than the Japanese women asleep with their men in her apartment. Her companion, a small but powerfully built Japanese man, was still awake. He was making them a small pot of tea.

She joined him at the kitchen end of her apartment, draping an arm around his muscular shoulders as he removed a kettle from the range and poured it over green tea leaves in a ceramic pot. They sat down together at a little table. She lit a cigarette and smoked as they waited for the tea to steep.

"When will he come?" she asked. They spoke in English.

"Not for three more days."

"You are sure?"

"It is what the Wolf has said."

The woman raised her hand to silence him from speaking further.

"What was that?" she whispered.

He had heard nothing, and told her so.

She walked to the window again, nonetheless. All was still quiet in the Ginza. The policemen had passed the building. They would return a few more times this way before the night was over.

She decided that she had heard nothing.

A man on the roof of her building watched as she left the window. He signaled to another man, who in turn signaled to two more.

Four men, two of them Americans, two Japanese, stepped through the darkness to the front of the roof edge. Silently, they let drop their rappelling ropes to a few feet above the ledge line of the new tenant's floor. They secured the top ends by hooking them into the steel railings.

Silently, the four made their way down the face of the apartment house, small steps at a time. Strapped to their backs were lightweight Uzi submachine guns.

Inside the apartment building, a platoon of Americans made their way to an upper floor where the Italian woman lived. The elevator shaft was adjacent to her apartment and they did not wish to arouse the slightest suspicion of their coming. Like the men on the roof, the men in the stairwells also carried Uzis.

"You saw nothing?" the Japanese man said to her when she returned to her tea at the table.

"No. I was mistaken."

She took another sip of tea. She thought she heard something once again.

When she looked up, she saw that he had heard it, too. He pulled a small pistol from his belt and advanced on the window, through the shadows.

She picked up an AK-47, one of three lying on a butcherblock counter, and followed him.

He waved to her, ordering her to wake the others. As she did so, the slumbering guests clutched at their weapons involuntarily. Their eyes fluttered open and cleared only after their hands were wrapped around AK-47s or Lugers, fingers set at the triggers. It was a discipline born of many dread nights, nights when a whimper or a cough could mean a life lost. They were guerrillas, and they were ready to make war on a second's silent notice.

One by one, the bodies in the room came to, stood up, guns clutched in hands.

Outside, on the ledge, the four commandos could hear the rustling; they knew they had lost their only real weapon, the surprise element. There would be death now on each side. Eyes widened and the sweat began to pour.

Commandos in the stairwells had reached their floor and were forming into flying wedge position at the door of the apartment, ready to charge through the barrier at the first crack of machine-gun fire. One of their number listened closely at the door. Something was different. The sounds of sleep had stopped.

A glint of light flashed on the barrel of a commando's Uzi—light refracted from a fog lamp in the Ginza.

The scream of attack from inside the apartment came from first one and then a dozen or more young throats.

Then the bullets sprayed.

The commandos rushed through the two windows at the ledge, their Uzis sweeping the room in a horizontal, side-to-side shower of bullets. Only the sound of dropping bodies told the commandos they had hit their targets in the pitch black of the apartment.

One of the American commandos felt fire at his throat and chin. A half-dozen bullets had made their mark. He made a futile attempt to stop the gush of blood flowing from his neck. He was thrown back by the force of the bullets, back toward the window. One more bullet crashed into his body, smashing his breast bone. He was thrown back wildly into the window, into the shards of glass and beyond. His balance and his breath and his strength at an end, the commando fell to the street, losing his life somewhere in the time it took for his broken body to hit the pavement.

The door to the apartment had burst open in that instant and the room filled with more commandos; the men with the Uzis poured into the darkened studio, filling it with the dull popping repeater rhythm of their weapons. One of them fell immediately, hit by the fire of the Italian woman. Her shouted revolutionary slogan betrayed her position. The burp of a Uzi sliced through her abdomen and she pitched forward, then down to the floor.

Someone, one of the Americans, shouted an end to the firing.

A light switch was found and flipped on. Twenty-four

youths lay dead on the floor of the apartment, most of them Japanese.

The American commando on the street below was surrounded by Tokyo police officers, with more on the way, running up and down the Ginza in the shadows made by a hundred windows suddenly gone light.

In the apartment, the only body removed was that of the commando felled as he broke through the door.

The other riddled bodies were left where they were. The living left the premises as silently as they had arrived.

...ANDORRA

Ben Slayton scrambled out of his bed to the safety of the stone floor. He heard the rifle fire again. Then again.

It was an almost leisurely sort of firing he heard, unaccompanied by return fire or the primal, savage screams of soldiers in combat. Could it be a firing range, Slayton wondered? He kept crawling toward the slits that were the windows of Sigrid's loft.

He raised his head over the edge of a slit in the wall. Though he could not immediately make out the meaning of what he saw below, he thought to look back at Sigrid. She had stirred herself and was now sitting up in bed, a sheet twisted around her thighs.

Sigrid's breasts were exposed to the chill of the morning air. The nipples were rigid. The light brown moss of her pubis glowed. Slayton was confused by his emotions, fear and lust welling in him simultaneously. He looked at her eyes and saw nothing more than a woman awakening to the unsurprising sights and sounds of her own home.

Below him, on the broad plain Sigrid had pointed out to him the night before, were a score or more men moving about in some manner of precision. The few who barked out commands, in French, wore *couvres-nuque,* cloth sun protectors at their necks.

A line of men fired carbines into the air, out over the drop-off at the limit of the plain, at the sound of a barked command. The shots echoed through the fog-shrouded mountain peaks. Slayton strained to hear clearly a chorus of voices as they chanted in French. He made out the words the third time it was called out:

"Honneur et fidélité! . . . Honneur et fidélité! . . ."

The ritual came to an end. Slayton watched the men as they closed ranks, turned from the plain edge and marched toward the castle. He could not see directly below him to the ground. The small army simply disappeared.

In her bed, Sigrid stretched and yawned.

Slayton stood up and returned to her bed, dropping down heavily beside her.

She didn't wait for him to speak.

"I lied to you," she said. "I do not live here alone. Today, you will meet my family. Today you become one of us."

Fourteen

WASHINGTON, D.C., 2:14 a.m., 16 March 1981

The night was hard for Hamilton Winship. Each night had been hard since Slayton's departure.

He hadn't slept this night, nor had he managed to rest more than five hours in a single twenty-four-hour period in the last month.

Slayton had been so cock-sure of himself, so certain he could pull off the mission alone. It was, after all, what Winship had wanted: a lone agent.

After all those years of waiting for the right man to come along, he had mistakenly assumed that his frustration would at last be ended; finally his great guilt at being impotent to see justice delivered would wash away in a burst of covert actions.

He had forgotten that the man he was waiting for, the man he needed on the outside while he handled arrangements from within, was a human being. A young man he would be sending out to face death, a young man of hopes and dreams. He was sick in the pit of his stomach.

Winship and Slayton, during their final hours together in Washington, had recognized their fate. They were remote soldiers fighting at the outer edges of a new world war, a manner of war never fought in all the bloody history of man. They would fight against terrorists who stalked the world, not merely some battlefield—invisible

111

warriors who wreaked their destruction often, sometimes preferably, on innocent people.

And their most dangerous enemy, they both knew, was always the enemy within. Those who furtively permitted even the assassination of an American President, those who would never raise their voices in unified outrage.

Slayton was out there somewhere. Not hearing from him, not knowing, wore down Winship.

They had decided on a brothel in Paris, not far from the headquarters of Interpol, as a place where Slayton could receive coded reports of Winship's findings. Otherwise, they were not to be in communication with each other.

Winship had told Slayton to move to Paris well before the date of President Reagan's trip to Japan. Slayton would have to decide, based on what he might discover at Andorra or elsewhere, whether to scrub the President's travel plans.

Now that the trip was only a week off, Winship's unease was increased. Had Slayton been killed?

Of course, there was that chance. He had seen many men killed in his years at Treasury—men he knew, men whose families he knew. This time it was different. Ben Slayton seemed something of a wayward son to him. He believed Edith felt the same.

He remembered calling him "that hippie" after their first meeting. He hadn't thought of that in a long time.

Edith slept peacefully beside him. He debated for a second or two on lighting a pipe. No, it would wake Edith.

The telephone rang and he wasn't surprised. Winship answered it before the first ring had stopped. Edith only grunted.

"Yes, Winship here," he said.

He was told of the slaughter in a Tokyo apartment building.

"All of them were killed?" he asked.

"Yes, sir."

"They are all as we were told they would be?"

"Yes, sir. Red Guards, every one of them."

"Thank you, Rodgers."

Winship settled back into the pillows he had propped up against the headboard and sighed, a long, satisfying whoosh of pure relief.

The Japanese know how to handle these matters, he thought. Move in quickly and quietly and eliminate the cancer. Winship could be satisfied that the presence of American agents would be kept from the press. The Japanese intelligence services were very cooperative.

Now he knew the President would be safe in his travels, even though he was still uncertain of Slayton. Perhaps their theory about the Wolf being the threat was incorrect, at least at this time. What possible connection could he have with the Red Guards?

Winship and other high-level American intelligence officials had been tipped to the quiet assembly of Red Guard terrorists in advance of President Reagan's still unannounced—that is, officially unannounced—trip to the Japanese capital. The source of the tip was European, and that was all Winship or anyone else knew of it. But it had proved right on the money. Right down to the last detail—the Italian woman and the studio apartment and terrorists brought singly to the premises so as to attract no attention in the vicinity of the Imperial Palace.

Now he would be able to authorize the advance teams of Secret Service agents to Tokyo. The President's trip could be on.

Winship fell asleep.

... *ANDORRA*

Sigrid pecked him on the lips and climbed out of bed. She crossed the room to a pile of jumbled clothing, the garments she tore off when she and Slayton first stepped foot in the loft. They had wasted little time. Now she just as efficiently pulled her clothes back on.

Slayton addressed her pale round buttocks, watching them disappear into denim confines.

"Those men are your family?" His voice was incredulous.

"My brothers in the struggle," Sigrid said.

113

"And why bring me into your clan, sister?"

She turned and faced him.

"You are a man of principle, as I said. I believe you will like us and what we seek to do with the world."

Slayton could barely contain himself. *My God, I've found him! I was right!* His thoughts reverberated loudly in his head.

"Suppose I don't like what you plan to do with the world? I don't know if I like the idea of anyone talking about taking action on a world scale. That sounds—"

"You will like us," Sigrid broke in. Then she smiled.

Slayton shivered inwardly. It was her accent more than the words.

"Just suppose."

"I do not suppose that. Now, get dressed and follow me. Come now."

She clapped her hands together. Slayton got up out of the bed and dressed, enjoying how Sigrid watched his body, wondering about all the men he had seen below on the plain. Was she the only woman here? By her appetite of the night before, he couldn't imagine that she was.

He followed her down from the loft, down a ladder leading to the ground floor he had entered last night. They picked their way around a pile of rocks massed around the entrance to an old corridor leading off the huge foyer of the castle column and proceeded, crouched over nearly double, down a blackened, dank passage leading to the open air.

Sigrid and Slayton stepped out into the plain.

He saw what had been darkened by the night, the rear portion of what remained of the castle. The plain formed a sort of courtyard, around which crumbled columns such as Sigrid's tower were grouped.

Slayton saw clusters of men standing in the entrances of the three other round castle sections. They appeared to be waiting for him to do something and they were not at all surprised by his presence.

He turned toward Sigrid, seeking explanation.

"You will walk out into the center of the plain, please," she said to him.

"Why?"

"To be tested."

"Look—"

"No. You look. You look up there."

Sigrid pointed to a parapet in one of the castle columns. Slayton looked up at the business end of a carbine equipped with a telescopic sight.

"You must take the test, you see," Sigrid said sweetly.

Slayton looked up at the sharpshooter again, then to Sigrid.

"Keep the bed warm for me, sister."

He turned his back on her and walked slowly out toward the center of the plain, understanding full well what it was like to have been a Christian among the lions in a Roman coliseum. He was to be this morning's entertainment. If he lasted until the end of the show, so be it; if not, his carcass could simply be shoved off the edge of the plain along with all the others Sigrid-the-spider-woman had lured up here.

For several minutes, Slayton was left alone in the middle of the plain. He watched the men and they watched him. He could hear them sizing him up, deciding how best to humor themselves with his demise.

Slayton breathed deeply. He tightened his muscles, then relaxed them, repeating this several times. Spreading his feet, he placed his hands on his hips. He shouted at the men in French, insulting their parentages.

Two of the men standing together strode toward him, dropping their revolvers to the ground as they neared, as well as their gunbelts. They held in clenched fists, however, nine-inch wooden batons, steel-filled.

Slayton waited until they were within three feet of him before he moved. Then, with a shrill cry, he seemed to leap straight off the ground, his legs somehow stretched out before him, his feet straightened at the ankles and pointed toward the hearts of his assailants like two sharp daggers hurling into their bodies.

The stiff toes of his boots caught each man in the chest, stunning them, knocking the wind from them and pitching their heads forward. They reeled on their feet as Slayton nimbly twisted in the air and landed on his feet and hands after the perfectly executed jujitsu strike.

Back on his feet and erect, Slayton rushed the men as they stumbled for their balance, as if intoxicated. He raised his right knee violently, then his left, giving each man a vicious slam in the jaw. They were now pushed backward, screaming. One man had caught his tongue between his teeth when Slayton connected with his hard knee. Blood poured from his lips.

Slayton pursued them now as they retreated. He stomped his boot heel on the tops of their feet, injuring the delicate tarsal bones.

His would-be assailants were now bobbling helplessly in their pain. The men waiting were shouting their encouragement to their comrades.

One man finally fell, covering his bleeding mouth with his hands. Slayton moved on the other man, managed to wrestle away his baton, chopped him on the throat with the rigidly held flat of his hand, and spun him around to face his cheering fellows.

Slayton then rammed the baton savagely into his pants, under his buttocks and out between his legs.

The injured Frenchman was given a hard shove and received the loud swat of Slayton's boot on his rear end. He managed four or five steps toward the line of cheering men before he stumbled, sprawling to the ground at their feet.

Then Slayton walked to the other man, still writhing in pain on the ground. He reached down, grabbed him by the hair, and cracked his head down on the hard ground.

With one hand full of the Frenchman's hair and the other gripped, viselike, around the tender cords below the thin skin of his neck, Slayton shouted to him in his tongue:

"Eat the dirt! Eat it! Eat it!"

The beaten man, his mouth full of blood and mucus, put his lips to the ground and groveled for a mouthful of the sandy mountain soil. Slayton yanked at his hair and turned his head. Satisfied that he had taken the soil into his mouth, Slayton pulled him to his feet and marched him to the line of his comrades, none of whom was cheering any longer.

Behind the line of men, Slayton noticed a comparatively composed and noticeably older man. This one was dressed in a fine uniform and he calmly smoked a black Tunisian cigarette.

Slayton had no time to study the man with the cigarette, the man who stood with his arm gently around the shoulders of Sigrid. His attention was drawn to the steel in his own back.

One of the men had inserted the razor-sharp tip of a knife into the small of his back. If Slayton resisted his command to move back into the center of the plain, a kidney would be slit open. Slayton marched.

When he reached the center, again, the man with the knife ordered him to turn around. Then Slayton was handed a knife of his own. The Frenchman squared himself and slashed the air with his knife, inviting Slayton to the fight, fair and square.

Slayton decided to take his time with this assailant, reasoning that the appearance of a hard struggle might end his test all the sooner. He knew it would be no contest. Slayton could have disarmed the man with a single swift chop from a foot or hand.

The Frenchman lunged in close to Slayton, slashing toward his midsection. Slayton sucked his stomach in, allowing only a rip in his shirt.

As the Frenchman's arm moved away, Slayton lurched, catching the tip of his knife against the top of the Frenchman's right forearm, opening a gash.

The Frenchman stepped back and licked at his wound, an evil threat forming in his eyes. He danced back and forth, parrying in and out, trying to open cuts in Slayton.

With lightning speed, Slayton again caught the Frenchman on the rebound, this time opening a wound on his chest. The Frenchman now flew at him in a berserk rage. It was what Slayton had known would come; he knew he must end the fight.

Slayton sidestepped the bull rush of the Frenchman. With his free hand, Slayton caught him full in the stomach.

His opposite elbow then slammed down hard on the back of his attacker's head. He heard the Frenchman's throat fill with blood as he fell to the ground.

Slayton was on top of him quickly. He pulled the Frenchman's knife away from him and flung it over the edge of the plain. Then he held his own blade across the Frenchman's throat, ordered him to stand, and marched him back to his starting point.

After releasing this third vanquished man, Slayton broke through the line and confronted the older man smoking the black cigarette.

Slayton paid no attention to Sigrid, though she stood next to the man who clearly was the leader, by dint of his age and bearing.

The leader nodded at Slayton, approvingly, but said nothing.

Slayton stunned him by saying, "I have the privilege of speaking to the Wolf?"

Fifteen

ANDORRA

Yes, he looked like the image of the grainy photographs he had seen in Winship's office, magnified photographs of the man, never identified, who was in Dealey Plaza, in Dallas, in November of 1963. But Slayton couldn't be absolutely sure. He also looked like quite a changeling.

He was of medium height, just under six feet. A man of middle years, perhaps nearing fifty-five. His age was the most difficult to detect. His physique was that of a twenty-five-year-old athlete, though his eyes had seen much of the world's horrors, too much for an athlete of twenty-five.

His hair was close-cropped, and he was clean-shaven. A thin line of scar tissue ran from the tip of his chin down under his jaw toward his throat. The memento of an old bit of combat, perhaps on the occasion of running across some band of murderous Bedouins while trekking across the breathless *hamada*—desert as hard-packed as superheated concrete, a place for devils to battle.

And this man was very clearly a devil. He had not a scrap of humanity in his expression. It was the look of a relaxed jackal, his appetite for flesh quelled, for the moment.

He wore the old Legionnaire uniform, his *kepi* gleaming white atop the black leather brim, red-fringed epaulets squaring off his shoulders. Above a small row of military decorations worn over his heart was the round shield of the *Légion Etrangère*. Slayton read the words, emblematic slogan of the French Foreign Legion: *Legio Patria Nostra* —the Legion is Our Fatherland.

Slayton knew full well, of course, that this was no authorized encampment of the Foreign Legion. He knew this was the lair of the Wolf, the international outlaw and renegade Legionnaire.

He would let the Wolf explain himself, however. He would bide his time, waiting until he knew how to end his menace. Or if he could end it. In his distinct favor was the fact that the Wolf had not the slightest idea who Ben Slayton was. Nor did he care. Evidently, he was interested these days in assembling his notion of what the modern-day Légion Etrangère should be, a force for reforming the world in the image of its self-proclaimed leader.

"Monsieur, will you kindly join me. Inside." The Wolf pushed open a small door at the side of one of the castle columns, and Slayton followed.

When he was seated, the Wolf spoke again to Slayton, who sat opposite him at a round wooden table at the center of a small room that had been fashioned into a wine cellar of sorts.

"It is early yet, but I wish to drink to your bravery even now at this hour," the Wolf said. An aide who looked to be Khmer appeared with a bottle and two goblets, which he set down between the two men.

When the bottle was uncorked, the Wolf spoke.

"An *appellation contrôllée* red called *Réserve Legion Etrangère*. Ha! These Legionnaires today. They all live at the home near Aix-en-Provence and they work on pottery. They make ashtrays in the form of the *kepi,* yes? And when they die, there are the funerals in the Legion's cemetery, full of lights and cypress trees at the edge of Mont-Sainte-Victoire. Ha!"

"The cemetery," Slayton said. "It was a favorite subject of Cézanne, was it not?"

"So, you are not merely a man who is good with his hands and feet. You are educated. You know of Cézanne."

"I know of many things. I don't know why I am here and I expect you're going to tell me. Now, please."

The Wolf chuckled and poured the wine. He tasted his, allowing it to roll about his tongue before swallowing.

Then the Wolf's eyes narrowed.

"I am a man who looks at your face," the Wolf said, his voice a cold grating sound, "and I decide what your name is to be. We are men who need new names. We have trouble with our old ones, our real ones. We have problems in our pasts we would rather forget, or at least rather not talk about.

"That is the way it is here. That is the way it was, in the old days of the Legion. Not today. The old ways are practiced only here, under my command.

"I select my men on the basis of their technical abilities today as well as their abilities at hand-to-hand, yes? You passed the first test. Now, what have you to offer me in the way of technical ability? You are an educated man."

"Tell me first why I should offer you anything."

"It is your choice, of course. You may offer me something or you may die. Your hands and your feet are not so fast as the bullet."

Slayton stalled, sipping at his wine slowly, infuriating the Wolf, whom he knew to be an irritable, impatient man; dangerous, to be sure, but weak where Slayton was strong.

"Speak to me!" the Wolf finally blurted.

Slayton grinned.

"You failed once before because of that temper," he said to the Wolf. "But only once. You have since carried out your work well."

The Wolf's face turned to stone. "Please tell me more," he said.

"You were part of an elite band of Legionnaires and you attempted a *coup d'etat* against Charles DeGaulle. You and your men, traitors to France, were marched out of your headquarters at Sidi bel Abbès in Algeria by the French authorities. You were to be imprisoned at Devil's Island.

"As you were marched out, on your way to a life in prison, you and your men burst into defiant song."

The color rose in the Wolf's cheeks. Slayton watched him react. The Wolf regarded his captive with new respect. How had this American drifter learned of his background?

"It was I," said the Wolf, "who led the singing. It was, of course, the song of the little sparrow, Piaf—*'Non, Je Ne Regrette Rien.'*

"Did you know it was I who began it?"

"Not until now," Slayton said, "though it isn't as important as the fact that you were the only man to have escaped the Devil's Island punishment."

"I killed my guards with my bare hands," the Wolf said. "Today, I might be able to do the same. I don't know.

"Tell me, how is it you know of my history?"

"I listen carefully. I know of the legend. In the city of Andorra, I connected the legend to a name. Simply the 'Wolf.' Tell me who you are."

Slayton correctly estimated the Wolf for a talkative man when the subject came to himself. What man wasn't, who held control of a private army?

"My life was something of the tragedy of the little sparrow herself. When my father left us—that was when we lived in Marseilles—there was illness and there were accidents that cost us what little money we had. My mother became alcoholic, I had a brother who stupidly was drawn into heroin use; he even had me using it for a time. Until I killed him.

"When that happened, I had to run. I had to live on the road, by my wits and little else."

"And of course, you discovered the Legion," Slayton said.

"Of course. Living on the run is living life on the seedy outer circle. It is living life without fascination, without interest in anything beyond the merest survival. Life is a flaccid world for a man who runs from his past. The Legion is the perfect answer, the perfect chance for new life, protected from an accountability to classic stupidities of one's youth.

"The Legion will save a man from many sorts of despair, my friend; the Legion will return a man's pride. Or, I should say, it did.

"We live now in a world of nations run by puny little runts instead of men. We live in a time when these whippets tell us that our national glories are no longer worthy, that we must as national policy recognize 'rights,' so-called, of inferior peoples."

"And is that why," asked Slayton, "you attempted to assassinate DeGaulle? Because he had presided over the independence of Algeria? Because he signed the cease-fire in 1962?"

"Yes. You are also correct as concerns my temper. I was discovered, you see, because my temper was so out of control that I spoke of my desire to murder DeGaulle, the man who would let Algeria go."

"But you never made that mistake again?"

"Never. If a man knows my mind and I think he may be dangerous to me by that knowledge, I kill him."

"You could keep your own counsel."

"It pleases me to kill." The Wolf let an evil smile play across his face. "And a man should not keep his feelings pent up inside him, do you not agree?"

"Would you care to get something more off your chest?" Slayton asked. "How do you manage to sustain this little army of yours?"

"I can tell you. Why not? You will either join with me or you will die, after all."

Slayton was quite sure he spoke sincerely.

"Cigarette?" The Wolf extended his pack of black Tunisians. Slayton declined.

"We have friends," the Wolf said, blowing a puff of the acrid smoke across the table. "Friends from the old Legion. These are men who have left to become important businessmen. Not only in France. In many countries of the world, including your own United States, my young friend.

"Our friends have certain mutual interests, a certain philosophy we here share. A philosophy of glory, of the survival of the fittest."

"And you oppose those who stand in the way of your philosophies?"

"Naturally. We are the Legion of old. We are kept as

123

the old Legion was kept. For those times when armies need to be dispatched to deal with irritations without any great moral warfare on the home front. Do you understand?"

"Murder, Incorporated."

"I beg your pardon?"

"An Americanism. Forget it. Go on, please."

"You said 'murder.' "

"Do you deny murdering people?"

"I do not deny killing weaklings or those who would allow the rule of weaklings. But you must know something about what you call 'murder,' young man. You must understand that there are interesting and instructive distinctions between killing and murder.

"We're taught that the Commandment of Moses—I don't know which one—reads, 'Thou shalt not kill.' But in fact, the literal translation from the Hebrew reads, 'Thou shalt not do "murder." '

"There is, you see, a point in law that further distinguishes. We call this homicide justifiable and that homicide unjustifiable. In Latin, it is *malum in se,* evil in itself, as opposed to *malum prohibitum,* something that is wrong only because there is a law against it."

Slayton's head was spinning. He heard what the Wolf had to say, understood it, but knew he was face to face with the most dangerous sort of man, a charismatic maniac. He knew Winship was very probably correct in his assumption that the Wolf was associated in some ugly way with those rogues of the C.I.A. who could easily be implicated in the assassination of John F. Kennedy. In fact, the Wolf was probably the assassin who got away, leaving Lee Harvey Oswald to take the full punishment. After all, it was only a year earlier that he attempted the DeGaulle assassination.

His talk of murder versus killing, his overblown attempts at rationalizing his own monstrosity, and his obvious support from a variety of men who were fascists in their own way added up to a certainty in Slayton's mind: the Wolf had been responsible for orchestrating the deaths of two members of the U.S. Congress and the attempt on the life of Vice President Bush.

There had been signs for years that someone among the world's terrorists would make some effort to unify guerrilla fighters the world over. It was the obvious future of warfare, short of nuclear holocaust. A beast no longer had the need of a huge standing army. He would need only a loyal group of fanatical brutes, willing to share in his booty, willing to live the life of a rich outlaw gangster, feeding off the voluntary or involuntary support of short-sighted industrialists and politicians. It was precisely how Adolf Hitler had organized himself.

"Sir," Slayton said, as the Wolf lit up another black Tunisian, "I am at your command."

The Wolf nodded.

"Of course you are, one way or another. But you still have not told me what you have to offer to me. We are all specialists here, you know."

"I offer you a working knowledge of military aircraft, you have seen that I am able to take down any of your men—"

"You are not who you seem to be!" the Wolf shouted, his fist slamming down to the table. "I will find out who you are."

Slayton felt the blood run cold in his veins.

Sixteen

ANDORRA

"Who is this American?"

Anthony asked it of Sigrid as they drove slowly down the narrow road from the castle into the city. She shifted into the lowest gear, easing the Maserati through a series of ruts.

"An interesting possibility."

"Did you sleep with him?"

She took her eyes off the road, a path, actually, made by some ancient herd of goats, and glared at him.

"If you dare say a word of your filthy suspicions—"

"You can't threaten me. If I was to say anything, you know he would kill you."

She looked away, back to the road, angrily.

"Do you remember Turin, my little *fraulein?*"

She refused to speak to him.

"Are you too overcome with tender memories, my dear? The memory of our little stop along the way? The inn outside of Trieste?"

She reached the highway and then turned to him, her voice loud and threatening.

"I never should have let that happen. You're a swine, Anthony. I tell you, I will find some way of getting rid of you. You don't have much reason to be smug."

Anthony laughed at her.

"Just get us to the bank, Sigrid. We'll finish our business as soon as we can and then . . . who knows? Maybe we'll have time for a noon-time rest before we have to head back."

The Wolf was without benefit of aides or guards. It was only he and Slayton, seated now in the Wolf's study. The Wolf had, however, a .45-caliber revolver pointed at Slayton's heart.

"Now, let me say this just once more," the Wolf said. "I find it hard to believe you're an itinerant television crate maker. Your talk is good. You're an educated man, both by the book and by the street. Someone taught you well. If you're an American government agent, be assured that I shall soon know. I have certain connections there."

"C.I.A.?" Slayton chanced.

The Wolf said nothing.

"Sure. You're C.I.A. Lots of people back home wonder if the Company is ever going to be on our side, which is a good question. Look, I'm telling you the truth. I'm not anybody's agent. And I withdraw my offer to fall in with you. I think you're stark, raving mad."

The Wolf stood up and walked to where Slayton sat. He clouted him on the side of the face with his revolver, then stepped quickly back. The Wolf had seen Slayton's speed, and was afraid of being overpowered.

"Listen, cockroach," the Wolf said, "I'll know soon enough. I have a man here with C.I.A. background. Yes. He'll have a look at you and then we'll see."

If it were true, Slayton knew his life wasn't worth anything. He quickly calculated that the Wolf's man must be the man who had poisoned Senator Samuels. It was one thing to fool a man like the Wolf, whose vanity and megalomania could be used against him; it was quite another to fool someone trained by the C.I.A. A spook was sure to spot him.

"And if I clear your next hurdle, what then? Am I taken into the club here? Or will you make some further claim against me? Can't you just accept the fact that I'm

128

an overeducated, burned-out old hippie Vietnam vet? I mean, that could be a fair candidate for the Legion."

The Wolf considered his argument. It had a sensible ring to it. That he couldn't deny.

"We'll wait here and we'll see," the Wolf said, glancing at his wristwatch. He lit another black Tunisian.

"Yes, we shall see. Meanwhile, tell me more about your plans to . . . what did you say you were going to do with your friends out there?"

"We're building a new order," the Wolf said. "A new order of valorous men. And women. We will assist those who should be running the world's important nations."

"How exactly would you accomplish this?"

"By demonstrating our capabilities, of course. Already, my friend, we have made impressive strikes. The country we are most interested in—yours, namely—has been shocked to its foundations."

Slayton doubted that the nation at large was unduly upset by the deaths of Barlow Hurgett and Richard Samuels, however they went. As yet, the nation was unaware of the Bush assassination attempt. The first two sorties into international terrorism were perhaps shakedown missions, Slayton considered, designed only to test one's own abilities and to monitor the retaliatory actions of the other side.

The Wolf would have to make his move on President Reagan if he was to make a mark in the world, if he was to impress terrorist organizations in other countries with whom he wished to ally. Anyone could kneecap an Italian ex-politician. It would take a real leader among terrorists to bring down an American President. Or so it might make sense to someone like Slayton.

Of course, the Wolf was someone quite apart from Slayton.

"I notice that Reagan is still in office," Slayton said. "I assume you mean to do something about that to promote yourself?"

"You are too insolent to be a good spy," the Wolf said. "Perhaps you are not, after all. Perhaps you are too insolent and too stupid, like most Americans.

"You ask about President Reagan. Let me tell you this: your people believe it is safe for the President of Hollywood to travel to Japan. And that is exactly what we wish them to think.

"So he will travel to Japan, as scheduled. Oh yes, we know of the schedule, even if most Americans do not. He will be able to leave the country.

"But the question is, will he be able to return?"

She had hit on a plan of action as they drove back from the city into the hills.

During the entire trip, Anthony yammered at her, nagged her about her meeting Slayton at the bar, demanded to know of any intimacies. God, the man was no better than the Wolf! Men wanted only to possess women. They didn't want to love them, to honor them; and they certainly wouldn't obey them. They only wanted to possess them, to show them off to their friends—other men.

Maybe the American was different. She had never spent any time to speak of with an American man. Perhaps Ben wasn't representative. What did it matter, anyway—a man's nationality? She knew only that this American, Ben, was a man for whom she had looked for a long time without finding. She knew that if given the opportunity and the time—time away from this dreadful prison life with the tyrant she once somehow thought so dashing, so exciting—she could fall desperately in love with Ben. In fact, she thought, she was already in love with him.

But there were two enormous obstacles: the Wolf and Anthony.

She had met the Wolf when she was only a girl in Hamburg, a student at the Polytechnic. The Wolf, who was using the name Rene Laclerc at the time, was much younger, too, of course. Still virile.

He was simply a man who spent a great deal of time in the public libraries when she met him, a seemingly wealthy man; at least, a man who didn't need to work for someone each day. Whenever she had to use the library, he was there, always reading from some ponderous work, as if he were on some desperate cycle of inhaling knowledge, as if deprived of books most of his life.

They would chat amiably in the library, not too familiarly; after all, she was German and he was French and there was still quite a social gulf to span. But in time, they were meeting for meals and drinks together in the pubs of Hamburg.

It was at these times he would spin his adventurous tales: the time he nearly drowned in *fesh-fesh,* the Arabic word, he taught her, for a desert sand so fine that it can suck you up like a swamp; a battle somewhere in Morocco, the French forces pursuing the Moroccan rebels for day after day, neither side having adequate supplies of water.

She remembered, as she drove, of that particular story, more for the strange delight in his telling it than the story itself.

". . . Three of us had been eaten by the desert jackals as we slept. We woke to find their bodies, and to find that the enemy had pulled out. They had a large lead on us. Later that day, we literally fell across them in the desert, never expecting we would," the Wolf, Laclerc, had told her.

"They had been set upon by the jackals themselves. Nearby was a well, left by nomads. We rushed to it. It was stuffed with corpses, Moroccan corpses. We never knew why. The water had turned crimson.

"All of us took our cups from our belts and drank the red water. We drank to our fallen enemy. And then we buried them, with their shoes off and their heads facing Mecca. A sign of respect to Islam and their combativeness.

"I shall never forget the words of our commander: 'This day, you have done honor to France.' "

It was this compulsion with honor and glory, two words the Wolf used frequently every day she had known him, that eventually replaced his passion for her. By then, however, she was traveling the world with him, to lands far from her small world of Hamburg, West Germany. She had no home except that which he made for her.

That would be no more, if the rest of the day went well for her. She might have a man to help her out of the increasingly insane and frightening existence in the Andorran mountains . . . and she might have someone to go to, someone special to her, if only he could be touched after so many years' separation by so vast an ocean. But . . . would he be insane, too?

Sigrid looked to the passenger side of the Maserati. Anthony leered at her. She spat in his face.

Slayton managed to read part of the letter on the Wolf's desk. The Wolf was rummaging through a bookshelf, searching for some volume of legal text to buttress a lesson he was giving Slayton at the moment. When his back was turned, Slayton stole a long glance at the letter, which he had earlier noticed—couldn't *not* notice—as the Wolf fingered it, occasionally glancing down at it.

Slayton read the final words of the piece, written in English, as they appeared to him, upside down:

". . . amazing the things you learn with a library card. Love, Edw."

The Wolf found his volume. Slayton sat back in his chair. His snooping had gone undetected.

"Here it is," the Wolf said. "The words of our enemies, with whom we will deal harshly when the time is correct, when we have our visibility and our consolidated power.

"Look, only last year, Charles Hernu, a 'defense expert,' so he says. Nothing but a Socialist party hack. He calls for the Legion to be abolished, even the weakened Legion that we know today. And of course, the Communists. They call the Legion an 'instrument of colonial conquest and repression of the people.' Lies!

"But the most hurtful of all our enemies' criticism comes from Antoine Sanguinetti. He says, 'Once upon a time there were the Three Musketeers, and the Pope had Zouaves. The Legion's time has passed.'

"This Sanguinetti will pay for those words with his life."

"And his death will be a killing rather than a murder?" Slayton said, mocking him.

"You will shut your mouth! You're a man on trial!"

"And you're a man who is mad."

The Wolf struck him again with the butt of his revolver. This time, Slayton managed to grab his wrist. He was nearly in position to send the Wolf flying over his back onto his own. But the door to the study opened.

Anthony scooped up the revolver, which had slid across the floor during the brief struggle. He shouted to Slayton, "Halt, or I'll shoot!"

Slayton stopped, released the Wolf.

"Thank you, Anthony. You have possibly saved the world a grievance. Now you may do me one more service, Anthony. I want you to take a close look at this man with me, the man you found trying to kill me. Talk to him if you wish; tell me if he is an American spy."

Anthony was both shocked and honored. He walked in a circle around Slayton. Sigrid, meanwhile, had taken a position near the Wolf and was whispering into his ear.

The Wolf's complexion went scarlet.

"Stop it!" he shouted. "Anthony, you are the traitor! Sleeping with my Sigrid!"

He waved his hand at Anthony, accusing him with his finger. Sigrid moved closer. She slipped a small pistol from her belt and put it into the Wolf's hand. In a rage, he pulled the trigger.

He caught Anthony in the bridge of his nose. His face was a bright blob of bone-spattered blood. He dropped instantly to the floor, a bullet fatally lodged in the front of his brain.

"What?" the Wolf shouted. He moved about the study, as if dazed. "What? . . . what? . . . what?"

Sigrid tapped Slayton on the shoulder. Never had he seen more pleading in a human face.

"You must, please . . . Ben, oh Ben, you must get away from this place. You must help me escape it, too. Here, finish it off." She took the small pistol from the Wolf's hand and gave it to Slayton.

Then she knelt over Anthony's fallen body. Near his pulpy head was the Wolf's own .45-caliber revolver. She picked it up in both hands and aimed it at the Wolf's head.

"Wait!" Slayton told her.

He crossed the room to her and took the revolver from her hand. She was quaking uncontrollably. Tears streamed from her eyes.

"Too much noise," Slayton said.

The Wolf stood, paralyzed. Saliva began flowing from one corner of his mouth. An eye went bloodshot. His temples pounded visibly.

"Your Maserati," Slayton said to her. "Is it outside, around the other column?"

"Yes."

"Go there. Take this with you." He handed her both handguns. "Don't let anyone see them. No one has come in here, so I don't think the shot from your pistol was heard outside this room. We have to rely on the quiet.

"Now move!"

Sigrid did as she was told, woodenly. Her plan was working. It was working! Soon she would be free!

Slayton approached the Wolf, who was oblivious now to anything real happening around him. He easily removed the small knife in a leather sheath hanging at the Wolf's belt. Then he walked the Wolf around behind his desk and helped him sit down.

He pulled Anthony's body to a place of concealment behind the desk. If someone were to look in from the doorway, all would appear normal. Then Slayton stepped behind the Wolf and ran the length of his knife blade into a lung.

None of the men milling about the plain outside had reason to suspect anything wrong had occurred inside the Wolf's study. No one had seen the two men argue. In fact, there had been a public display of respect when the men first met.

Slayton walked calmly, deliberately, around the inner edge of the plain, to the side of the first castle column. He crossed over the moat bridge to the Maserati.

"Move over," he said to Sigrid. "I'm driving."

She obeyed him. As she shifted, she caught sight of one of the castle guards, standing high atop a section of the castle tower, his carbine raised to the hip level. He was watching the two of them in the car, watching their hurried movements as they believed they were out of sight.

"Ben," she yelled as he fired the engine and learned the feel of the gear box, "we've got to move, fast. Up there!"

Slayton didn't look. He could guess her meaning and her urgency.

He clamped down hard on the accelerator, spinning the wheels wildly in the dust and stone surface of the mountain road. The shots were finding their mark on the rear deck of the car. He held the wheel firmly, swerving the car to the right and to the left, trying to confuse the marksman with a fishtail course.

"Faster! It will go faster!" Sigrid shouted.

Slayton punched the floor pedal and the Maserati leaped over small piles of loose rock and bits of pine branches strewn over the granite. The damaged car crashed back down to the road, but Slayton held the powerful car to his course, preventing its going out of control.

The shots kept coming. And Sigrid kept screaming. Then he heard her no more above the low, fierce growl of the Maserati's engine. He couldn't look at her, though he imagined the worst. The driving required his total effort.

When he finally reached the highway, Slayton put the Maserati at flat-out speed. Then he was able to glance over to Sigrid.

He saw her shining blonde hair flying lushly in the wind. She was so terribly beautiful.

And dying. Blood trickled from an ear. Her neck was bent backward, like a broken doll.

He braked the Maserati and brought it still at the side of the highway. Sigrid's eyes still had some life. Her final energies were put into words. Slayton strained to hear them:

"My Edward . . . my . . . Oh, Ben, stop him . . . the power plant . . . Oh, stop my baby . . ."

Life left her then.

She had almost made it to freedom, to normalcy.

And Ben Slayton had escaped death.

This time, he thought.

Seventeen

Slayton, numb and shaken, stepped off the DC-10 Air France jet at Orly Airport. He carried no luggage, which he knew would make the customs agents suspicious.

He needed to clear French customs as quickly as he could. It was only two days before President Reagan's trip to Japan. Winship would be going crazy with worry, wondering when Slayton would make contact via the Parisian brothel.

He took a deep breath and proceeded from the plane to the baggage carousel in the Customs Building, where the passengers from Andorra began milling about, waiting impatiently for the conveyor belts to begin spitting out their bags and parcels.

Slayton stood slightly behind a family group. A father, his overweight wife, and three children. They would be sure to have plenty of luggage.

He stood with his hands in his pockets to keep them from sight. They were trembling. He was more nervous about the prospect of stealing someone's suitcase than he had been about slipping a knife into a man's back in his own office. With the man's own knife!

And he was trembling because of Sigrid. By now, some-one would have found her body. He could do nothing but pitch her out of the car. He had rolled her body into a

137

culvert at the side of the highway into Andorra. A woman he had made love to only . . . how many days ago . . . how many hours? What was the day? The time? Slayton felt quite faint. He closed his eyes and bit down hard, forcing blood up into his head and face. The last thing in the world he needed just now as to keel over.

At last the luggage began appearing, making its agonizingly slow crawl down a chute onto the carousel's conveyor belt. Blue bags and brown, black and yellows. Fortunately, one could tell pretty much what might be inside a bag by seeing it. In the old days, everyone—men, women, and children—traveled with the same brown and black square valises. Today, a man carried brown or black, women and children owned the colors. Thanks for small favors.

The man in front of him lifted a passing suitcase from the carousel, and, just as Slayton expected, set it down beside him and watched for others. This time around, it was entirely unsuited to his purpose, which was to clear customs with a bag full of jockey shorts, socks, and a change of shirts. When a standard brown bag came up and the man set it down with the four others he had already hoisted off the carousel, Slayton deftly picked it up and walked away, quickly.

He had his American passport ready, along with his visa papers, as he approached the customs agent. The functionary rubber-stamped his passport a few dozen times, for whatever reason customs agents are possessed by, and ordered the suitcase opened.

"Hope you don't find any contraband," Slayton joked, just to prove he was a regular sort. The customs agent kept his sour face.

Slayton clicked open the fasteners and opened the lid. To his utter amazement, the suitcase was filled with a sea of Spandex undergarments, definitely for a woman big enough to be told by a cop to break it up while standing on a street corner all by herself.

The customs agent twitched his upper lip. His mustache, a little bit of a thing, rode up and down as if caught in a fit of apoplexy.

His eyebrows shot up into the air, requiring a fast explanation from Slayton.

"You see," Slayton began to say in English. He corrected himself and continued in French: "You see, my wife and I always fly separately. She's coming in on the next flight. We have matching bags and, would you believe it, I took hers instead of my own. Well, I don't suppose it makes a whole big difference, does it?"

The customs agent was sputtering, but Slayton sensed he didn't see anything as ludicrous as his stealing someone else's luggage. Slayton quickly considered that his best route out of the situation was to make it even more ludicrous. He fished out a pair of oversize panty hose and held them up to his chest.

"Doesn't suit me, does it, Pierre?" he said to the agent.

The man bought it. He waved him through the customs gate, giving a Gallic shrug of his shoulders, meant to convey his long-held mystification over anyone and anything American.

If he had the time, or the heart, Slayton would have delayed his return to the States for several days' rest and relaxation in the French capital. But on this trip, even the spectacular beauty of Paris was not enough to keep his mind off the events of the past few days.

As his taxi took him down the Avenue Grand Armée, beneath the Arc de Triomphe and on to the Champs Elysées, Slayton grew increasingly depressed. At the madness of the Wolf, whoever he was; at the horrible loss of a woman with whom he had been intimate but had not known, a woman to whom he owed his life, a woman he had only a few hours ago thrown out of an automobile like a sack of rubbish.

He shut his eyes to the beauty of Paris.

Slayton had given the address of the bordello to the driver. It was in the Montparnasse district, south of the Eiffel Tower and Les Invalides. He slumped back into the taxi's seat, overwhelmingly exhausted.

Facts swam through a mind too wired with recent action and split-second decisions to find rest and peace .. con-

139

nections and discrepencies . . . try to fit the facts together, to make all the connections as tidy as possible.

. . . Congressman Barlow Hurgett was assassinated in Munich, more than likely by the Wolf, who was more than likely some manner of C.I.A. operative who conspired to assassinate President Kennedy; Senator Richard Samuels died in Turin of a massive coronary, more than likely brought on by tobacco poisoning, more than likely performed by the man he knew as Anthony, a suspected C.I.A. operative or former operative; the attempt on Bush's life was carried out by someone posing as an American backpack tourist, and Slayton himself had prevented the London murder try; the Wolf and Anthony were dead . . .

. . . The young American tourist who supposedly lost his means of support to pickpockets in London was someone named Edward Folger, an obvious alias with an obvious dummy address; presumably, Winship would be checking on that matter from the States while Slayton was off risking life and limb in Europe; Winship was convinced that the Wolf was ultimately gunning for President Reagan, though the Wolf himself had said something cryptic about it . . . what was it he had said?

The taxi stopped abruptly at a row house near the Edgar-Quinet subway train station in Montparnasse. Slayton paid his driver and lumbered out of the back of the cab, leaving the stolen valise inside.

As he climbed the stairs of the stoop, the driver called to him: "Your bag, sir! Don't forget it!" Slayton obligingly reclaimed the suitcase full of girdles and corsets and whalebone brassieres. Would he ever be rid of them?

Yes, he suddenly realized. Yvonne would take them.

When he reached the door, Slayton tapped out the signal he had used twice before. Yvonne's brothel owed its existence to the courtesy of Interpol protection. Hers was a convenient center for message exchanges.

Three taps, wait; three more, wait; then two. A small peephole flap opened and Slayton could see the heavy blue-black mascara of Yvonne's right eye. The good one.

"Hiya, toots!" Slayton greeted her.

140

She took him in her huge, fleshy arms, more the hug of a great-aunt who kisses a lot than that of one of Paris' busiest madames.

"Come on in, Benji boy, come right on in. We'll get you a drink and a real good time while you're here in the city of light, okay?"

Yvonne's French-accented English was more Brooklyn than French. *C'est la vie,* Slayton thought as he followed in her wake, which was the most appropriate way to describe walking behind Yvonne's girth. He was offered a seat on a huge, overstuffed pink couch, decorated on one end by a tall Nubian woman in an ivory negligee. Slayton didn't even perspire when he saw her, and wondered if he would ever be a well man again.

"Now, Benji boy," Yvonne said, after settling her great hams on a settee opposite the couch, "I got some news to tell you, you know?"

He stared at her glass eye, the one that was slightly off-kilter every time he saw her. It slipped downward, as if it were made of steel shavings attracted by a magnetized bosom.

"I am to tell you—"

She stopped as one of the girls walked in, a trayful of drinks in hand. She bent over, revealing a pair of very white breasts tipped in pink. He took a glass of champagne and looked dully at the girl's wares.

When she left, finally—blessedly, as Slayton was beginning to worry himself sick about lack of appetite—Yvonne continued:

"The bad boys of Tokyo have been terminated with extreme prejudice and the coast is clear for Sir Jellybean. You're to hustle on home for a week off with pay, assuming all is connected on your end."

Slayton remembered then what the Wolf had said about President Reagan's travel plans: "Your people believe it is safe for the President of Hollywood to travel to Japan. And that is exactly what we wish them to think . . . But the question is, will he be able to return?"

He jumped up from his chair, spilling champagne over his clothes. The Nubian slid down the couch toward him, murmuring, grabbed him inside his thighs, and tried coaxing him back to the seat.

"No," he said quietly, firmly. He looked at the hurt expression on the prostitute's face. "Sorry, but no. No thanks."

His mind was clicking, suddenly come alive in spite of his fatigue and his sorrow.

He rushed from the room, toward the door and the street. Yvonne called after him:

"You forgot your suitcase, Benji boy! Your suitcase!"

He turned around and blew her a kiss.

"It's a present for you, with all our love! I'll catch you in a Maidenform ad. Bye-bye!"

And he was out the door.

At the nearest telephone booth, he attempted the impossible: the use of a public telephone anywhere in France.

He hailed a cab, hopped to the nearest police station, and instructed the operator to dial the special emergency number of Winship's office.

After several minutes of crackling sounds and after becoming accustomed to the echo in the trans-Atlantic telephone cable wires, Slayton and Winship spoke.

"Just answer these questions, Ham, as briefly as you can. There may not be a whole lot of time."

"Right. Go ahead."

"The Edward Folger kid. What's the word?"

"Nothing much. He was supposed to have been from Yonkers, up in Westchester County, New York . . . my home grounds—"

"Briefly, Ham."

"Yes. Well, that's about it. He had a phony family set-up, of course. Good enough to fool the embassy in London, but that's it. The only thing we turned up with his name on it was a library card. Hard to believe he's connected to the others."

Slayton's muscles tightened. This horror wasn't over. Not by a long shot, so to speak.

"The President," Slayton said. "He's leaving exactly when?"

"We're making the announcement tonight. That is, the White House is making the announcement."

"When, Ham?"

"Forty-eight hours."

Slayton cursed.

"Listen, Ham. The Wolf is terminated."

"Sounds like a mission accomplished," Winship said, jovially. "When will I see you?"

"Later than you think. I hope not too late."

Then Slayton clicked off.

Eighteen

BUCHANAN, New York, 19 March 1981

Buchanan is anything but typical of the glut of small factory towns at the upper reaches of Westchester County along the Hudson. It is neither gray nor grim, nor inhospitable to plant and animal life because of the bilge of industrial pollution in the air and water of other towns less fortunate than Buchanan.

After all, Buchanan had a nuclear power plant. A clean, safe source of abundant energy.

It allowed Buchanan to exist as a picture-postcard town in a part of the nation Washington Irving memorialized in his *Tales of Sleepy Hollow*. The village itself was perched between a pair of heavily forested mountains and the wide Hudson River, a soul-invigorating respite from Manhattan, with a real general store, a string of little taverns that sold mostly locally brewed ale, church spires, and a town hall straight out of Central Casting.

The nearby Indian Point Nuclear Power Plant saved little Buchanan from financial obliteration back in the late 1960s, when it opened and provided a wealth of much-needed jobs in town. The Schenley distillery had just closed, throwing most of the Buchanan wage-earning class out of jobs.

As an appreciation for Indian Point, the Buchanan police chief and all his men wore the atom-splitting insignia of the village's biggest employer as its proudly chosen shoulder patch.

A few malcontents in Buchanan suggested that the village formulate some sort of evacuation plan, just in case their town some day became another Three Mile Island. Majority ruled, and there was no evacuation plan.

Up above the village, an old scratched Chevrolet idled in a cul-de-sac off a narrow, winding road. The heater tried to keep the driver's feet warm, if not his hands and fingers, as the young man behind the wheel hunched over his notebooks and papers.

A bitter wind off the Hudson made his fingers stiff and cold. It was hard to turn the pages, the more than three hundred photocopied pages of instructions, floor plans, and diagrams.

Around the bend in the road, at the edge of a thick forest, was the entrance to the Indian Point Nuclear Power Plant, the pride of Buchanan. The young man sat in his car less than a mile away. He finished a sandwich as he went over his plan for the hundredth time.

He had been tipped off about emergency evacuation drills for the plant guards and workers, and he knew that today it would be held at noon, precisely eight minutes away. He'd better step on it.

During the drill, one of which he had observed earlier via binoculars, all guards and employees would be withdrawn from their posts. All he had to do was drive up to the gate minutes before the drill bell sounded and say he had an appointment with the superintendent of operations, whose name he had learned on the ruse of having a letter to mail and needing to know the correct spelling of his name and his correct title. He planned to use a press pass he had had printed down in the city. Simple, he thought. So simple it was bound to work.

Once inside the grounds, he would head straight for the nuclear reactor building and go to work.

Ready to roll. He put the Chevrolet into gear and headed down the road.

In minutes, he turned onto the four-hundred-yard long blacktop access road toward the main gate of Indian Point, only slightly worried about having his bag searched. He would simply say it was a camera. He *was* a reporter, after all. He looked the part, a combination of the characters Animal and Rossi he had studied on the "Lou Grant" television show.

A guard signaled him to stop, stepping from the guardhouse and walking toward the Chevrolet. The young man rolled down his car window. "I'm a reporter," he said. "There are some brass hats I got to see today, for my paper." He handed over his press credentials, which the guard glanced at and returned.

"Who you want to see today, son?" the guard asked.

"Tom Emerson, superintendent of operations."

"You say you're with what paper?"

"The *Times. The New York Times.*"

"Yeah, okay. You wait here a minute."

The young man was nervous. Only two and one-half minutes until noon. He wanted to be well inside the grounds by then. Was something going wrong?

The guard sauntered back to the car after making a telephone call to someone.

"I seen one piece of ID," he said. "You got any more on you?"

The young man produced a billfold full of credit cards, all in the name of Edward Folger. Every one a forgery.

He remembered the precaution he'd taken of slipping a White House press pass into his bag of burglary tools in the event someone called him on it. He would simply fish out the White House press pass and impress the hell out of the yokels. It had worked before. How could anyone tell a press pass was counterfeit? How many people had ever seen a White House press pass?

"Okay, I guess you're a regulation gentleman of the press, all right," the guard said. "They let you into the White House and everything, huh?"

The young man made a joke, even though he was anxious about the time.

"Guess security guards aren't invited to the White House, right, Mac? Ever since that guy came across the

147

adhesive tape at the Watergate complex, Presidents have been nervous around you fellows."

The guard laughed.

"Okay to go now?" the young man asked.

"Oh, they're coming for you," the guard said. "You wait right here and they'll come for you in the limo. Mr. Emerson is waiting."

.-. . Wait a minute. This wasn't supposed to be happening. Behind him, in the distance somewhere beyond the chilly mist, he heard the noon church bells from the village. But there was no drill siren blown at the plant.

He saw a long black car pull up. A man in a suit emerged and gestured to him.

"This way. Mr. Emerson is waiting," the driver said.

The young man had no choice. He walked to the limo in a trance. What would happen to him? He was sickened by the thought of failing . . . him . . . twice.

In another minute—now it was six minutes past the hour—the young man was seated in a large executive office. Its occupant was not in. A secretary had seated him and given him coffee. He thought back to the secretary in London. . . . He was going through a nauseating sense of *déjà vu*.

Thomas Emerson walked into the room. It was the alias of the day for Benjamin Slayton.

"Good afternoon, Mr. Folger," he said. Folger hadn't given him his name. "I've been waiting to see you."

The lines of exhaustion that had set around Slayton's eyes for the past thirty hours he'd waited for Folger's appearance disappeared. This would close the case and Slayton knew nothing more invigorating.

Folger coughed.

Slayton picked up a pencil from the desk top and held it while he sat on the edge of his desk, facing the young man who looked so much like a newspaper reporter.

"I killed your father, the Wolf," Slayton said.

Folger blinked. The color went out of his face.

"And your mother is dead, too. She died saving my life and saving the world from you and your father's terrorists."

Folger made some gurgling noises in his throat.

148

The pencil that Slayton held was especially sharp. Slayton's eyes kept dancing from Folger's face to his hands.

Suddenly, Folger leaped from his chair. He was fast, maybe faster than Slayton. A stiletto knife dropped into his hand from its clip up inside his shirt sleeve. The blade was making its way for Slayton's throat.

Slayton darted out of the path of the stiletto. His cheek and right ear were caught by the tip of the knife. Slayton wouldn't allow another wound. The young man was good. Too good. He'd been trained by his father, the best of his day.

Slayton moved swiftly with the pencil. It stabbed upward, below the young man's jaw, up through the soft palate and deep inside his brain.

Edward Folger crumpled to the floor.

Nineteen

Ben Slayton wanted to be alone for a few days before making his verbal report to Winship. Guessing that he'd been through hell and back, Winship had allowed the luxury.

Today, he was coming, though, and Ben fussed about his place. Winship was a first-time visitor to the farm, and his boss on top of that.

It was late afternoon. The light would be good in the library and so that was where Slayton prepared for the meeting. He set out a coffee and tea service, biscuits and brandy, and set a fire ablaze.

"Turning into an old cunt," he muttered. "Look at me. Some guy's coming to my place and I'm setting out the doilies."

He heard the sound of gravel crunching on the driveway and he poked his head around the corner to catch sight of Winship's arrival. He came alone, in a silver Lincoln. Perfect.

Slayton received him stiffly and thought how odd it was that the two men were shy with one another after what they had hatched and carried out. For an hour, they sat in front of the fire making small talk. The enormous implications of the mission could not be rushed conversationally.

As Slayton let the brandy slip down his throat, then another and another, he made believe the older gentleman sitting next to him before the fire was his own father. He missed him.

"Are you feeling better?" Winship asked for the fourteenth time, at least. Winship, too, was becoming quietly lubricated.

"Yeah. Still a little rocky, that's all. Killing that boy!" Slayton shook his head. "And losing Sigrid."

"Your country owes you—"

"I don't want my country knowing," Slayton butted in. "This is dirty business. All right, I'm willing to do it. But I'm not willing to crow about it, okay? Besides, a lot of it was luck. Just plain bloody luck."

Winship nodded.

"There was no other way?" he asked after a few moments' silence.

"I don't see how. No particular loss, the Wolf and Folger. They were nonpersons. They don't exist.

"But Sigrid, poor Sigrid. I'm not sure that she thought of herself as any more real than her husband or her son.

"But she was real, Ham. If she had lived instead of me, she would have found herself. And I think she may have found her son here in the States, too. Maybe she could have stopped him, short of killing him."

Slayton wiped his eyes and poured himself another brandy. Winship held out his own snifter and was refilled.

"When did you begin putting it all together?" Winship asked.

"That's hard to pinpoint. I put myself in the stream of things, trusting for luck. And that's exactly what happened. The small bits began adding up to the real plot. I played my hand and Sigrid played hers . . . maybe that's when it began, meeting Sigrid.

"Her behavior was so ambivalent, so damn curious. She's cold as ice, then she's a goddam tigress in the sack, and then the next morning she's got me in a situation where the Wolf's men could have killed me. She was loyal to the Wolf, but afraid of him; loyal, but unsatisfied with him. She was confused, maybe afraid of going mad herself, as mad as the Wolf.

"There was the letter I saw on the Wolf's desk, too. It was signed 'Love, Edw.' The love of a son for his father. That's how such a letter would be signed. Sigrid was quite clearly the Wolf's woman. It wasn't such a difficult conclusion to make that she was also Edward's mother. And that was part of her trouble, too.

"She must have known that the Wolf, Edward's father, was prepared to sacrifice their son in the name of this 'new order' business. How can a mother reconcile revolutionary sacrifice and the certain death of the product of her own womb?

"So I was on hand and she saw me as a way to get herself the hell out of Andorra, don't you see? Maternal instinct at work. She was trying to get to her son, Edward. Bloody luck. I learned what I had to learn at her tragic expense.

"That letter on the Wolf's desk also mentioned the 'amazing' things to be learned at a library. When I spoke to you by telephone from Paris, you mentioned record of a Westchester County, New York, library card in the name of Edward Folger."

"What arrogance," Winship humphed. "He used the same name for a public record as he did when he ran the London bomb attempt."

"Like father, like son. The Wolf left the Piaf clue in Munich—'Non, Je Ne Regrette Rien'—and he had Anthony and Sigrid leave the same calling card after the murder of Samuels in Turin. What's that but calling attention to yourself? What's that but arrogance?"

Slayton was on his feet now, thinking out loud on the process that led him to the incredible conclusion he hadn't even yet verbalized. Not to himself, not to anyone.

"Your message left at Yvonne's, in Montparnasse, said the 'bad boys of Tokyo' had been 'terminated with extreme prejudice,' making the President's trip safe to plan. The Wolf had told me that our confidence in Reagan's safety was exactly according to his plan.

"Don't you see? The Red Guards massed in the apartment in Tokyo was merely a ruse. A red herring, if you will excuse the pun.

"The Wolf was allied with them and yet he used them, sacrificed them. He tipped us, probably through one of Anthony's connections with the C.I.A., and we wiped them out. Killing them, we naturally thought the 'coast was clear,' as you said in your message left with Yvonne."

"Brilliant," Winship said.

"Yes, isn't it? Savage and brilliant at the same time. A feint on one continent to cover the actions of guerrilla war on another."

Slayton wet his lips with brandy, then continued.

"I remembered Sigrid's dying words about some 'power plant,' and that's when it all clicked together.

"In order to position himself as the preeminent terrorist leader in the world, the Wolf had to pull off something absolutely incredible, something theatrical, something that had never before been attempted by terrorists.

"You see, the kneecapping days are over. Nothing will be simple any more.

"The Wolf, after some shake-down runs—that was the sniping in Munich, the poisoning in Turin, the snafu attempt on Bush—decided that only the most complicated maneuvers would serve his theatrical purpose.

"The plot was . . . and this is really unbelievable . . . to sabotage the Indian Point Nuclear Power Plant, or threaten to leak radioactive wastes, and thereby prevent the absent President of the United States from returning to this country. That's what the Wolf meant when he said to me, 'But will he be able to return?' "

"That *is* unbelievable," Winship said.

"Why? Because it never happened?"

Winship had no response. Slayton was correct. What other explanation could there be?

Slayton sat down. Sank down, actually. He was still exhausted, mentally and emotionally, if not physically any more.

"And from this you knew to take the Concorde from Paris to New York and to get up to Indian Point without a second's delay?"

Slayton sighed.

"I knew that the nearest nuclear power plant to Westchester County, New York, was Buchanan. Indian Point. I knew, too, that government classification procedures regarding the nuclear industry is, to put it charitably, schizophrenic.

"The classification system is one that government and industry have for a long time used to conceal the dangers of radioactive contamination and plutonium loss—I give you Three Mile Island in Pennsylvania and the A-bomb in India, maybe Pakistan as well, probably Israel and just possibly South Africa—and at the same time fill the public bookshelves with enough data to lead a college sophomore by the hand in the design of a bomb. It's a system that hides safety defects in nuclear power plants and at the same time makes them open season for madmen, employees with a grudge, and terrorists.

"If we had some leadership in this country, some President, say, with vision beyond next Tuesday, we might cure our schizophrenia.

"When I got to New York, I went to the main library in the Westchester County system, at the county seat of White Plains. Sure enough, I found what I figured would be there—the goddam blueprints for a terrorist, practically an invitation to walk right into Indian Point and take it over.

"I knew then that I had no choice but to play my hunch. I had no choice but to get up to Indian Point and take over the top man's office, in this case someone named Emerson who was called the 'superintendent of operations.'"

"And?"

"And wait. That's all we could do. Wait for some offspring of the Wolf—and Sigrid—to make his move. The security was on extra alert. Discreetly alerted, to be sure. We didn't want a panic. Luck again. Bloody luck.

"I could only figure that Edward Folger would waltz in completely 'legit,' as they say. After all, he had all the guidance our government could provide. There was no reason for muscle. Of course, I suspect I surprised him just a tad."

Winship shook his head. "We're all lucky, I should say, that you just happened to know a thing or two about nuclear power plants and the idiotic classification system that goes along with them," he said.

"I live in the world, Ham."

"Thankfully."

"None of that, I said." Winship yawned. "Listen, Ham, you have to remember one thing in this business: the bad guys depend on our being an open society, which means it's up to us good guys to keep up with the latest possibilities spread out all over the newspapers and in the libraries and all. We ought to take a tip from our enemies. Two of the best tools in antiterrorist work are library cards and newspaper subscriptions."

The two men enjoyed a laugh. And then another drink. But there was one more sobering question.

"Ben," Winship asked, "do you think the organization left behind by the Wolf, those lunatic Legionnaire masqueraders, will survive as a threat to the United States?"

"Maybe not that particular bunch. I would assume—and we'll be finding out from Interpol shortly, I expect—that they all fled with the winds from Andorra.

"But we know they're allied with terrorists the world over. The only message we gave them here was that we have their number."

Winship considered Slayton's words. He knew that Slayton now thought as he did. Winship spoke for both:

"This hardly ends it. Our message means little compared to the one given us. A message of clear and present danger."

MYSTERY...SUSPENSE...ESPIONAGE...

THE GOLD CREW
*by Thomas N. Scortia
& Frank M. Robinson*   *(B83-522, $2.95)*
The most dangerous test the world has ever known is now taking place aboard the mammoth nuclear sub *Alaska*. Human beings, unpredictable in moments of crisis, are being put under the ultimate stress. On patrol, out of contact with the outside world, the crew is deliberately being led to believe that the U.S.S.R. has attacked the U.S.A. Will the crew follow standing orders and fire the *Alaska*'s missiles in retaliation? Now the fate of the world depends on what's going on in the minds of the men of THE GOLD CREW.

DOORS
by Ed McBain   *(B91-937, $2.50)*
Meet Alex Hardy. He can plan and execute a robbery with consummate skill. He can seduce a woman with equal skill. But now he is faced with the most beautiful woman and the most difficult job he has ever encountered. Bone-chilling tension.

THE FRENCH ATLANTIC AFFAIR
by Ernest Lehman   *(B95-258, $2.75)*
The S.S. Marseille is taken over in mid-ocean. The conspirators are unidentifiable among the 2,000 other passengers aboard. Unless a ransom of 35 million dollars in gold is paid within 48 hours, the ship and the passengers will be blown skyhigh. A first-class ticket to excitement.

YESTERDAY'S SPY
by Len Deighton   *(B31-014, $2.50)*
Two friends who spied together. But that was in another time and another place — now they fight on different sides. A spellbinding tale of deceit and terror in a world where political reality destroys the most hallowed allegiances.

RECOVERY
by Steven L. Thompson   *(B93-482, $2.95)*
The year is 1982. Max Moss—a daring ex-racer on a specialized American rescue team—is perfect for the death-defying chase in a superspeed car for the recovery of a secret U.S. plane forced down in East Germany by Russian fighter pilots. Everyone is against Max and his partner as they use their wiliest resources to bring the plane's super-secret, biocybernetic device back to safety.

MEN OF ACTION BOOKS

DIRTY HARRY
By Dane Hartman

He's "Dirty Harry" Callahan—tough, unorthodox, no-nonsense plainclothesman extraordinaire of the San Francisco Police Department... Inspector #71 assigned to the bruising, thankless homicide detail ...A consummate crimebuster nothing can stop—not even the 'law! Explosive mysteries involving racketeers, murderers, extortioners, pushers, and skyjackers; savage, bizarre murders, accomplished with such cunning and expertise that the frustrated S.F.P.D. finds itself without a single clue; hair-raising action and violence as Dirty Harry arrives on the scene, armed with nothing but a Smith & Wesson .44 and a bag of dirty tricks; unbearable suspense and hairy chase sequences as Dirty Harry sleuths to unmask the villain and solve the mystery. Dirty Harry—when the chips are down, he's the most low-down cop on the case.